KASH

STAR-CROSSED ALIEN MAIL ORDER BRIDES

SUSAN HAYES

ABOUT THE BOOK

What do you do when your planet runs out of women? Send for takeout, of course.

Kash knows he'll never be allowed to claim a mate. A lifetime of military service has left him too battle-scarred and broken to be considered for the off-world mating project his rulers have created to save their people.

His job is to make sure the more fortunate males get to Earth to retrieve their mates. All he has to do is pilot the ship, stay undetected, and keep an eye on things from orbit. It should be the easiest mission of his career...until he lays eyes on the one thing he never expected to find. His mate.

This book contains a hopeful romantic who is giving up hope, and a soldier who is about to discover that love doesn't obey orders, and it can't be bound by rules.

SUSAN HAYES

Kash (Book #3 of the Star-crossed Alien Mail Order Brides Series)

First E-book Publication: November 2017

Cover Design: crocodesigns.com

Editor: Dayna Hart

Published by: Black Scroll Publications

ISBN: 978-1-988446-22-6

As always, this story is dedicated to my Mum and Dad, for their love and support of their sometimes-crazy daughter, and to Karen, who is the 'sister of my heart,' and a dear friend no matter how many miles are between us.

This story is also for Jenny C. for sharing a story that turned into inspiration in a very tight pair of shorts.

1

———

"This was supposed to be an easy mission!" Kash muttered to himself as he drummed his fingers on the edge of the console that controlled his ship's systems. All he had to do was maintain orbit around Earth, keep the *Firebrand* off the humans' primitive tracking systems, and wait for his charges to acquire their mates and return to the ship. It should have been simple.

Simple had taken a steep dive into the heart of a star shortly after the mission started. Joran, heir to the throne of Pyros, Crown Prince, and a royal pain in the ass, had decided to leave his ship early, ditching his contingent of bodyguards along the way. The future king was currently wandering the city of Vancouver alone and unguarded because apparently, he couldn't tell the difference between the royal gardens of Pyros and the threat-infested streets of this primitive world.

He slapped a hand down on the console and

opened a communication channel to one of prince's guards, audio only. They were on the planet below, looking for their missing charge.

"Yes, Commander Denza?" Guardsman Tarjen answered almost instantly.

"Tell me you've found him."

"No, sir. Not yet."

The drumming started again, faster this time. "Do you have any idea where he might have gone?"

"No, sir. He teleported out and programmed the system to erase the coordinates once he rematerialized. We're currently scanning for him, but it would appear he's switched off his locator."

"Where do you think he might be headed? It's not like he's ever been to Earth before. We're not even supposed to be in this part of the galaxy. His only reason for being here is to locate his mate. I suggest you start by figuring out where she is right now and ascertain if the prince is with her."

"Keth is already looking into that. We believe she is at her place of work, but we have been instructed not to approach her until contact has been made. Additionally, her workplace is in a heavy traffic area. There's nowhere nearby we can teleport without being seen."

That was one of the many problems with this *simple* mission. They didn't have permission to be here, and they were operating in total secrecy. The humans had no idea they were being visited by aliens, and it had to stay that way.

"Find the nearest safe location and make the rest of the journey on foot. I'm going to attempt to contact the prince again. If he doesn't respond soon, I'm going to come down there and kick his royal ass myself."

"Yes, sir!" Targen didn't bother to hide his amusement at Kash's statement.

They had all served together. Joran and his guards as fellow soldiers, and Kash as their commanding officer. Targen knew Kash meant every word of his threat. If the prince didn't report in soon, he'd be wearing Kash's boot-print on his ass.

He hit another button and opened a channel to his second charge, Vadir Rahal.

"Checking up on me, Commander?" Vadir owned and ran an intergalactic corporation. As one of the richest and most powerful men on the planet, he wasn't used to reporting to anyone. Not even for his own safety.

"That's more or less my entire job for this mission. What's your status?"

"My match has responded to the email, and I'm communicating with her now. Things are progressing. I have every reason to believe she will meet me for the evening meal at the designated location. Everything is going according to plan."

"That's good to hear. Do us all a favour and keep it that way."

Vadir chuckled. "Judging by your tone, I'd hazard a guess that Joran is already doing his own thing?"

"Something like that."

"This is why you should have taken me up on my offer to work for me instead of the royal family. I actually listen to the people I employ. Not to mention, I pay far better."

Kash snorted. "Ask me again after this mission is over. If anything happens to the prince, I'm going to be looking for a new job."

If he failed in this mission, he'd lose more than his job. He'd fought hard to be recognized on his own merits instead of relying on his family's influence. A lifetime of hard work, loyalty, and sacrifice had earned him his current rank. All of that was in jeopardy if this mission didn't go as planned.

"Joran can take care of himself, and so can I. Don't worry so much, Commander. We'll be back on board with our females before you know it. It's really a shame we can't initiate formal contact with this species. I could make a fortune just selling them environmental regulators and weather control satellites."

"Don't even think about it."

Vadir sighed. "I know. I know. Stick to the plan. I still haven't forgiven her Highness for doing this to me. I don't have time for a mate right now. I've got deals to make and a business to run."

"Not even you can ignore a royal decree, Vadir. When the king commands us, we must obey."

Vadir signed off, then, and Kash was left alone with his thoughts. His fingers started drumming on the edge of the console as he wondered what he'd done to make the Gods hate him so much. Not that his life was one of hardship or despair. He had made his own way in the world, made his family proud, and had gained the the trust of the most powerful family on Pyros. But pride was a poor companion, and duty was no replacement for a mate and a family.

He'd accepted that there was no mate for him on Pyros. It was a realization that many males had faced. With seven males born for every female, the odds simply were not in his favour. But then, when the scouts had discovered that compatible matches existed elsewhere in the galaxy, he'd dared to hope again.

He should have known better.

Only young, fit males from important and influential families were even considered for potential matches with the human females. Logically, it made sense. Those families had the means to fund this endeavour, and the power to keep the attention of the Inter-Planetary Council focused elsewhere. Young, healthy men would make good fathers and be able to protect their mates and younglings. Logical or not, it had still been a bitter draught to swallow.

Even if the mission was successful and the matches were later opened to other males, he would never be considered. He was past his prime, and no female would want an aging, battle-scarred veteran when there were so many handsome young males to choose from.

The Gods had chosen another path for him, one of solitude, loyalty, and the honours that came with a life spent in service to the crown. It was enough. It would have to be. With no chance at a mate or a family, his career was the only legacy he had.

———

Gwen pulled the last batch of brownies out of the oven and then looked around the kitchen in dismay as she realized she was out of room. Every inch of countertop and her small kitchen table were already in use. She popped the brownies back into the oven and scrambled to transfer the chocolate chip cookies from their cooling trays to an old-fashioned cookie tin that had once been her grandmother's.

As she stacked the cookies in tiny towers inside the battered and dented tin, she recalled the countless times she'd done this with her Gran. Back then, baking had seemed like magic. Carefully combining ingredients, watching them come together in the ancient mixer, then the pouring of batter and the careful placement of each ball of dough so that none of the golden, crispy edges would touch when they were done.

When she was feeling down, Gwen baked. It was comforting. The familiar scents, the routine of it. If she closed her eyes, sometimes she could almost hear her Gran quietly humming and feel the old woman's warm, loving presence. It soothed her, and for a little while, the world would be a good and peaceful place again. Today, she needed that.

The rain pattered against the kitchen window, loud enough to make her glance up and wonder how her two friends were faring. Hopefully, wherever they were, their dates had them out of the weather and were treating them like queens. They deserved it.

When there was enough space cleared, she popped the lid onto the cookie tin and went back to the oven to rescue her brownies. Without thinking, she reached in and grabbed the glass pan with her bare hand.

"Shit! Ow, shit, dammit." She yelped in pain, dropped the brownies, and dashed to the sink to run cold water over her burn.

"Good job, idiot." She scolded herself as she waited for the stream of cold water to ease the sting. It was a clear sign from the universe that it was time for her to stop baking and go to bed. She should have stopped hours ago. In fact, she had...for a little while. Lisa had come home from work and found her baking up a storm. Like the dear friend she was, she'd done what she could to cajole Gwen out of her dark mood. The levity had only lasted as long as Lisa's presence, though. When Lisa had headed out to meet her mystery date, Gwen had falling back into her funk.

Still holding her hand under the tap, she selected one of the still-warm cookies from its rack and munched on it while surveying the damage. The floor was strewn with chunks of brownie, and the glass pan was sitting upside-down with a massive crack showing across the bottom. She'd have to toss the whole mess out.

She started to cry, hot tears scalding her face as she looked at the mess on her floor. The ruined pan might as well have been named Gwen. She was as old and broken as it was, and she was being tossed aside, too. Her boss had given her the news today. The second-hand bookstore she'd worked at for years was closing down. The books she loved would be sold off, and the job she'd held for ten years would be gone.

On top of that, the same dating service that had provided her two best friends with their dates for the night had sent her a rejection email. She hadn't wanted to sign up in the first place, but Lisa had insisted, and between the wine and the ice cream, Gwen had given in. The Star-Crossed dating service specifically said it was for young women, though, and at thirty-five, she'd worried that she wouldn't make the cut.

Sure enough, at the same time her friends were being matched with drop-dead gorgeous guys, she'd been sent a politely worded letter informing her that she wasn't a match for anyone in their database, which was geared toward a younger age bracket. It was official. Just like the glass pan, her best days were behind her.

Maybe she should have agreed to go out with Shane, a customer who had been hanging out at the bookstore for months while he was 'between jobs.' He never bought anything, he just thumbed through the books, one hand in the pocket of his faded, too-tight shorts that puckered across the front and left nothing to the imagination.

He kept asking her to have a beer with him, but she'd always declined. Maybe it was time to stop fooling herself. Maybe Shane, with his nicotine-stained fingers and his awkward ways, was the best she could hope for.

How the hell had her life come to this? She'd always dreamed of having a family someday. Of sharing her life with someone who thought she was beautiful despite her curves. Yet, here she was, standing in her kitchen eating cookies alone on a Friday night with nothing to show for her life but an almost empty bank account and a job that was about to disappear.

She let herself wallow in self pity for three more cookies and then she made herself stop. Eating her feelings and moping wouldn't change a damned thing. All that would happen was she'd wind up feeling guilty about eating too much, and the cycle would begin again.

She dried her hand and carefully checked her fingers. Thankfully, there wasn't any real damage. Just a pair of small blisters that would only take a few days to heal. The way her day had gone, she could have wound up sitting in an emergency waiting room for hours.

"Ice and aloe, a baker's best friends." She broke off a piece of aloe from the plant on her windowsill, treated the burns with it, and then went to work cleaning up the mess on the floor. It wasn't easy to do one-handed, but she managed.

It was late by the time she finished cleaning up. The sugar rush from the cookies and brownies she'd nibbled on had faded away, leaving her tired and emotionally drained. She tossed the thawed-out ice pack back into the freezer and picked up her phone to check the time. Almost eleven, and no word from either Maggie or Lisa.

Unease and worry slithered into her chest and coiled around her heart. They should have checked in by now. The three of them set up a system years ago. Whenever one of them went out on a date, they'd check in to let the others know they were okay. Once when they arrived, and again when they were heading home. If things were going really well, they'd text or call and update on where they were heading next, and if they'd be out for the night.

Things were clearly going well for both her friends or they'd have sent a message by now. Should she act like a mother hen and call them for an update? She rejected that idea right away. Calling would be intrusive. She could text, though. She fired off a quick message to them both and hoped they wouldn't think she was overreacting. She just wanted to know they were safe before she tried to get some sleep.

Kash paced the floor of his quarters, too agitated to sleep. The prince had been located and was safely back on his private shuttle with his newly-acquired mate. That was the only thing that had gone right since Joran and Vadir had arrived on the planet. Both males were in the thrall of the Scorching, the mating fever that affected every Pyrosian when they first met their true mate. It shouldn't have been possible. Their matches weren't even the same species, but it *had* happened, twice.

That wasn't the end of the surprises, either. The prince had informed him that his mate did not live alone. She had not one but two friends who would notice her absence. How had that detail been missed? Their presence here was a secret, and they were breaking more than a few laws being in this part of the galaxy at all. First contact with a race as early in their development as the humans was completely forbidden. Because of that, the human females selected as matches were supposed to be unattached and easily removed without causing suspicion.

He smacked a hand against the hull. "We make plans while the Gods laugh."

It would be approximately two solar cycles before the newly mated pairs would be free of the effects of the Scorching. There was no way either female would be returning home until then. He needed to keep an eye on both residences and make sure that no one noticed Lisa or Maggie's absence. If they did—. Flames, what was he going to do if that happened? He couldn't do much from up here, and his orders required him to stay in orbit, overseeing everything. He wasn't supposed to get involved unless things were dire.

If the Gods were feeling generous, then the rest of the mission would go smoothly, and nothing else would go wrong. Something told him that wasn't going to be the case.

"Computer. Prepare two micro-drones for surveillance on the planet's surface. Urban setting. Maximum stealth mode."

"Confirmed. Destination?"

"Two different destinations. Target the home addresses on file for the human females matched to Vadir Rahal and Joran Pyros. Monitor and record any activity at both locations."

There was an unusually long pause before the ships AI spoke again. "Please reconfirm destinations. Data is in conflict with command given."

"Identify error."

"Home addresses on file differ, but coordinates do not."

"Details, computer. Give me the damned details."

"There is a minor variation between the two addresses, but both residences exist in the same structure."

He ran a hand through his hair and resisted the urge to try and punch a hole in the hull. "They live together? You're telling me that out of an entire city, the database managed to match two females who know each other?"

"I cannot confirm their social bonds based on current data, but statistically it seems likely the two females are acquainted, Commander."

"Display the two addresses side by side on wall monitor one, then display all data collected on the females in that building on wall monitor two."

It didn't take long for him to see the problem. The address was numeric, but the last character was a letter, instead: 1665-A and 1665-C.

The Spark. The Scorching. And now the revelation that Joran and Vadir's mates were already acquainted. The Gods were in fine form today.

"I don't get paid enough for this. I swear after this mission is over I going to seriously consider working for Vadir," he muttered as he turned to look over the data now displayed on the second monitor.

"Computer, why are there three names being displayed? I asked you to show me the information on Vadir and Joran's matches."

"The Commander is incorrect. You asked me to display information on all the residents of that building."

A headache blossomed behind his eyes, adding to

his misery. "Where did you get the information on the third female?"

"The Star-Crossed database included her information. Gwen Hudson was rejected as a potential match, but her information is still on file."

There were three of them. And the third one knew all about the Star-Crossed dating service. She would have to be dealt with before the others were transported to Pyros.

"Show me her file. Pictures. Data, all of it."

Information filled the monitor, but Kash didn't see it. All his attention was on the image the computer had placed at the top of the screen. A goddess stared back at him. Why was this beautiful, dark-skinned, lushly curved female dropped from the program?

He hadn't realized he'd spoken aloud until the computer responded to his question. "The female was determined to be past the prime breeding age for humans."

She was too old? He stared at her picture, unable to see any sign of infirmity or age. Her jet-black hair fell in tight spirals around her smiling face, and her skin was a warm, deep shade of brown that he'd never seen before. She was breathtaking. If she was an example of the females that were being rejected from the matching program, then the ones responsible were doing a great disservice to the males of his world.

"Send the drones to target location. Have one patrol the perimeter and have the second one enter the building and record all activity. If the inhabitant shows signs of becoming concerned or agitated, alert me immediately." He wasn't holding out much hope that the beauty on the planet below had no connection to the females already claimed by their Pyrosian mates, but he wouldn't take action until he had to. If the three were friends, it wouldn't be long before Gwen Hudson started to worry. When that happened, he'd have to do something, likely something that went against his orders.

Hopefully, by then, he'd have some idea what that would be because nothing in their mission plan covered this contingency. He was going to have to make things up as he went along.

He drummed his fingers against his thigh as he stared at Gwen's image on the monitor.

So much for simple.

2

———

His second officer messaged him after what felt like only seconds of sleep. The habits of a lifetime of military service had him on his feet before he was even fully awake, and he answered the call on the wall monitor before it chimed a second time.

"Report."

"The micro-drones are reporting activity at the target site. I checked, your subject is awake and appears worried. She's pacing and appears to have visited what we believe are the living quarters of the two females with Vadir and Prince Joran."

It was the middle of the night for this part of the world. There was no other reason that Gwen would be awake at this hour. She must have realized her friends had not returned home yet. He was going to have to go down there and handle the situation...somehow. Things had just gotten dire.

"Prep shuttle two, and continue monitoring subject." He was about to end the call when another thought struck him. "And put a damper on her communication devices until I get there. If she contacts the authorities and tells them about the dating site, this mission is going take a terminal dive straight into the nearest star."

Kash signed off and went to pull a fresh uniform out of his cubby, then stopped. He couldn't show up at Gwen's door dressed like that. The black and orange uniform of a Pyrosian military officer was designed to stand out, and that was the last thing he wanted to do while covertly visiting a planet they weren't supposed to be anywhere near.

"Computer, scan your database and have an Earth-style outfit manufactured to my measurements. Something casual and discreet. And make it quick. I'll pick it up from Supply on my way to the shuttle."

"Confirmed."

They had added a small number of templates for clothing and basic devices to their manufacturing stations in order to equip Joran, his guardsmen, and Vadir with everything they needed for their missions to Earth. It wouldn't make what he was about to do much easier, but he'd take any advantage he could get. If he didn't deal with the third female, then the mission was at risk. Of course, going down to the damned planet at all was a risk, too. He had never defied orders before and he didn't like doing it now, but he had no other choice.

He geared up quickly and headed to Supply to gather the rest of what he'd need. He donned the clothing, strapped a teleportation device to his wrist, and slipped his communicator into the pocket of his pants. The material was heavier than he was used to and the fit was alarmingly snug. How in the hell did human males fight in such constricting clothing?

There was one other accommodation he had to make. Instead of wearing his blaster on his hip, he slipped into a more discreet shoulder holster and covered it with a black jacket of simulated tanned animal hide.

The officer on duty checked her notes, gave him a quick once-over, and nodded in approval. "You look quite human, sir. No one should notice you at all."

He chuckled and offered the female a rare smile. "I'm not sure if I should be insulted by that or not."

Her golden eyes widened. "No insult intended, sir. I just... it's amazing how similar these aliens are to us. I've been reading the files, and well, I've got unmated brothers back home. This mission might mean they have a chance to find their mates someday. I hope whatever it is you need to fix down there, it works out alright. For all of us."

She drew herself to attention and brought her right arm across her chest in a sharp salute. "Good luck, sir."

He saluted her back, turned, and headed for the

shuttle hangers with her final words resonating in his ears. He was going to need more than luck to make this work. He needed the goodwill of the Gods themselves. Not that he could count on that, considering their sense of whimsy was the reason for all this chaos.

Gwen couldn't sleep.

It was after one in the morning, and they still weren't home. Not so much as a text message from either of them. She'd tried calling, but all she got was a "the number you are trying to reach is temporarily out of service," message. Her emails and texts had gone unanswered, and there wasn't a single post on either of their social media. She'd gone full stalker-mode and hadn't been able to find a trace of either of them.

She left her suite and climbed the stairs to Lisa's place first. She knocked on the door and called out several times, just in case she'd missed her friend's return home.

Satisfied that Lisa wasn't there, she hiked back down to the main level, then made her way downstairs to the basement, where Maggie lived. No answer there, either. Not that she'd expected there to be, but she wanted to be sure before she took this to the next level. It was time to call the police. There probably wasn't much they could do, but she'd spent enough time in foster care to know that when someone was missing, the sooner the search started, the better.

Back in her suite, she decided there was one more thing she should do before calling the cops: call the hospitals. She sat down at her computer and searched for the phone numbers she needed, jotting them down on the back of a takeout menu.

Her hands were shaking as she picked up her phone to call the first number. Which would be worse, finding out Lisa or Maggie was there, hurt...or confirming that they were out there somewhere, still missing?

She was so distracted by her worries that it took her a few seconds to notice that the call wasn't going through. *Weird.* The damned thing had worked twenty minutes ago when she'd tried to contact her friends for the hundredth time.

The battery showed more than eighty percent power, so what was the—no cellular service? She held the phone under her desk lamp so she could see the readout better. No service. How was that possible? For what she paid every month, she should get service at the bottom of a well in the middle of Antarctica.

Irritated and exhausted, she stood and started wandering around her suite, hoping for at least a single bar of connection. Nothing. She felt a stab of panic. What if Maggie or Lisa was trying to get a hold of her right now? The landline! She grabbed the list of numbers and left her suite again.

The others had laughed at her, but she had insisted that they keep a landline in the house for emergencies. This definitely counted as an emergency. The black phone sat out in the hall, close to the front door where any of them could use it. It was covered in thin layer of dust, which was a testament to how long it had been since it had been used.

She lifted the receiver and started dialling in the first number, then froze as she heard a footstep outside the front door. Were they finally home? Who was it? She waited in silence, hoping for the sound of a key in the lock, but instead, there was a sharp triple-rap on the door.

Disappointment and concern welled up inside her. If it wasn't Maggie or Lisa out there, who was it and what did they want this late at night? Her grandmother had been fond of say that only bad news was delivered after midnight. She set the phone back down in its cradle. "Who's there?"

"Ms. Hudson? I have information on the where-abouts of your friends, Maggie O'Hara and Lisa Woods."

A harbinger of doom's voice should not sound that sexy. She felt an immediate stab of guilt for even thinking that. What was wrong with her? "Are they alright? Where are they? Why haven't they called?" she blurted out the questions in a breathless torrent before she even had the door unlocked.

"They're safe and unhurt."

"Oh thank the stars—." She got her first look at the man standing at her door and words failed her.

He was huge. Not merely tall, but broad and muscular, too. He looked like he was built to do violence, and the scar that slashed across his right cheek only added to that impression. Something about him spoke of military training, too. The way he held himself, maybe, or the fact that his dark hair and beard were immaculately trimmed.

"May I come in?" His voice was as hard and gruff as the rest of him.

"You're not from the police department." She held her ground, her hand still gripping the doorknob. This was a stranger, with no uniform or badge to identify him.

"No. I'm not. But I do know where your friends are. If you allow me to come inside, I can explain."

Her need to know what had happened waged a brief battle with her sense of self-preservation and emerged victorious. "Come in. It's too chilly to stand on the doorstep and talk, anyway."

He gave her a heated look that made her heart do a slow somersault in her chest. "You are not dressed to be outside."

That's when she finally remembered what she was wearing. Or more precisely, what she wasn't. All she had on was an oversized t-shirt that barely came to mid-thigh. Worse, it had sparkly pink unicorn eating a cupcake emblazoned across the front of it.

She uttered a muffled squawk of embarrassment and folded her arms across her chest, hiding part of the cartoon figure. "You're right. Follow me, I'll get dressed, and you can tell me what the hell is going on."

She retreated inside, and he came after her, his long strides eating up the distance between them. She moved faster, her bare feet hitting the floor at a borderline jog. The sooner she could grab something to cover herself up, the sooner she'd have answers.

The human female was scared of him. She wasn't the first one to react that way, but this time, it bothered Kash. The lovely, curvy little female was the first human he'd ever seen face to face, and part of him had foolishly hoped for a different response.

Kash was used to others reacting to him with unease and even fear. Even before the scars, many had found him intimidating. Since he'd been injured, though, it had gotten worse. His scars were a reminder to the other Pyrosians that they were no longer the strongest force in the known worlds.

As their population shrank with each generation, the other races and factions had slowly taken notice. Raiders and pirates grew bolder. Shipping lanes that had been safe for hundreds of planetary orbits were attacked more frequently, and in the past few years, even the Pyrosian fleet itself had been targeted. He'd been injured in one such attack.

He followed her into the structure, trying hard not to stare at the way Gwen's sparse covering hugged the curve of her hips and ass as she walked. He would not allow himself to be distracted by her beauty. She was human, and therefore forbidden to him. She was a problem that had to be dealt. Nothing more.

"What's your name? Where are my friends? Are they really alright?"

He blinked at her steady stream of questions, not sure where to begin answering them.

When he didn't say anything, she tossed a worried look over her shoulder. "Please, tell me again that they're okay."

That, he could do. "You have my word that your friends are unharmed. They're with two males I know well, and they would never allow anything to happen to someone in their care."

"Then why aren't they answering their phones? I've been out of my mind with worry."

"Your friends' electronics are likely not in service." It was part of the plan, to make it easier for Joran and Vadir's ships to remain undetected, and ensure that their matches could not make contact with anyone and reveal the presence of aliens on this planet.

He followed her down the hall and through a doorway and was immediately struck by a sense of comfort and warmth. Mismatched furniture filled the main room, but it was covered by handcrafted blankets and quilts in bright colours. Nothing about it resembled home, but that's what it felt like; familiar and welcoming.

"How did you know that I was getting an out of service message when I tried to contact them?" Gwen pointed to another room, one filled with large appliances and the lingering scent of something delicious. "Please wait in the kitchen. Help yourself to the cookies or the brownies. They're in containers on the table. I won't be long."

"I know your friends' location." He walked into the kitchen and inhaled deeply. His stomach rumbled in response, reminding him that his last meal had been some time ago.

He wandered over to the table and looked over the array of tins and plastic containers arranged neatly across it. He opened a canister made of dented metal, and the incredible aroma grew stronger. Inside were stacks of baked goods, and he lifted one out to sniff at it. It reminded him of a confection his mother used to make when he was a youngling. He took a cautious bite and groaned in surprised delight as the flavour filled his mouth. It tasted even better than it smelled.

He opened more of the containers and found a large number of the tasty disks as well as squares of something dark and rich looking. He was relatively certain the squares were the brownies she'd offered him, which meant the disks were the cookies. His language training hadn't been as extensive as Joran and Vadir's, but so far, it seemed sufficient.

He had sampled a brownie and was eating another cookie by the time Gwen reappeared. She had covered her bare skin in loose-fitting clothing that hid her body.

He didn't like it.

"Now that I'm properly dressed, please tell me where my friends are. When are they coming back? What's happened to them?"

"Which question would you like me to answer first?"

She pursed her lips, and her gaze fell to the floor. "Sorry. I babble when I'm upset. I'd like to know your name, and then I want to know what happened to my friends."

"My name is Kash." He only gave her his first name. Mentioning his rank would cause more questions. "Your friends are with the males they were matched with on the Star-Crossed Dating service. The last I spoke with Joran and Vadir, things were getting..." he scratched at his scar as he struggled with his English, looking for a tactful way to tell Gwen what was happening.

"Were getting what?"

"Heated."

She glanced up at him, eyes wide. "You don't mean —God, you're blushing. You do mean that."

He stiffened. "I am not blushing."

She uttered a breathy laugh that made his balls tighten.

"Your ears are red, so you are blushing, at least a little. I'm sorry, I shouldn't be laughing. I'm just so relieved to know they're okay. They're more than friends, they're like family. The only family I have. It's just been such a horrible day, and then they didn't come back, and I thought something had happened to them."

"What happened to you today?" The words were out of his mouth before he even knew he was going to speak.

"I found out I'm losing my job. I mean, I'm not fired or anything, but the store is shutting down. Then Lisa and Maggie both got dates for tonight and I..." She stopped talking, her teeth closing on her plump lower lip.

"What else happened?"

She shook her head, setting her dark curls bouncing. "It's nothing. Really. Just a bad day that ended with a baking spree and a burned hand."

"You hurt yourself? Show me." Burns were something his people were very adept at treating. When a Pyrosian couple mated, they unlocked their ability to manipulate fire. While each couple was immune to the flames of their mate, that immunity did not extend to anyone else who might be within range.

She extended her hand to him, palm up. "I already treated it. I'll be fine in a day or so."

If they were aboard the *Firebrand*, the medical center could treat her in a matter of minutes. It was a sharp reminder that the humans were still a fledgling race, with a great deal to learn before they were ready for contact with the rest of the galaxy's residents.

"What did you treat it—" he stopped talking as his hand cradled hers and a cobalt-blue spark arced from his hand to hers.

"Did you see that spark? It didn't hurt, but it was so bright!"

"I saw it. Very strange." That might be the biggest understatement of his life. He had just experienced the Spark; a sign from the Gods that this female was his true mate. It wasn't merely strange, it was incomprehensible. He didn't have permission to claim a human female. Flames, he wasn't even supposed to be on this damned planet.

"What were you asking me a moment ago? Did you want to know what I treated the burn with?" Gwen asked.

He looked at the small blisters and reddened skin of her fingers. It had to be uncomfortable. He didn't like the idea of his mate being in pain. "I did. These still look painful."

"It's not that bad." She dismissed his concern with another shake of her head. "I soaked my hand in cold water and dressed it with aloe vera gel. From the plant over there. I'll be fine."

His mate had treated her injury with plant sap?

Unacceptable. He ignored the outraged voice. She wasn't his mate. She couldn't be. It was forbidden.

She withdrew her hand from his, and he had to fight the impulse to grasp it again. It had to be the Scorching; the mating fever that possessed all of his kind at the moment they found their mate.

"You need to take better care of yourself, *kaheya.*"

She frowned at him. "I can take care of myself just fine, thank you. And what did you just call me?"

His control was slipping already. "In my language, it means little one. I meant no offense by it."

All the warmth in her eyes vanished as she moved away from him. "I'm not little, though. Not even close. And what language was that, anyway? I've never heard anything like it. Your accent is unfamiliar, too." Her eyes narrowed. "I think I want to speak to my friends, now. I need to be sure they're okay."

"You cannot speak with them at the moment. As you already know, they're out of communication range, and are...otherwise occupied."

Gwen crossed her arms across the lush curve of her breasts and glowered up at him. "Either find a way for me to talk to them, or I'm going to call the police."

"I cannot let you call the authorities, Gwen Hudson. There is too much at stake." He was aware that the action he now considered ran counter to almost every order he'd been given. Every order but the one that mattered most: protect the mission.

And claim my mate. The second thought came

unbidden but too strong to ignore. Honour and duty had always been his focus. They defined his life and gave him purpose. Now, there was another force driving him. Her. There was only one way he could think of that would fulfill both duty and desire, if only for a few stolen moments. He offered her his hand. "Come with me, and I swear to you I will answer all your questions."

She stared at his hand, clearly at war with herself. "You want me to go with you? It's the middle of the night, and you're a complete stranger. A strange one at that. Why should I trust you?"

He squared his shoulders and gave her the truth. "My name is Kash Denza, Commander of the Pyrosian star cruiser the *Firebrand*. I swear on my honour that no harm will come to you while you're with me."

"Not good enough." Gwen shook her head and gave him a look that pierced his soul. "I've known too many honourless people. Swear on something else. Something precious to you. Then maybe I'll believe that it's safe to go with you...and everything else you just claimed."

Her courage was intoxicating. He had announced that he was an alien in command of a starship, and she hadn't so much as flinched. "My honour is precious to me. But if you need more then here it is. I promise you on the life of my mother and father that you will be safe."

The silence stretched out between them for so long

he started to wonder if she would reject that vow, too. Her gaze stayed locked on his, her expression one of careful consideration.

Finally, she gave a sharp exhalation and nodded. "You're serious. Holy shit. This is real, isn't it? You're from another planet."

"I am from Pyros, as are the males with your friends." He extended his hand to her again. "Come with me, and I'll show you." Once she was on the *Firebrand*, she wouldn't be able to alert anyone to what was happening.

"This is crazy. Stuff like this only happens in the books I read. Big, handsome alien commanders don't just arrive on Earth and ask someone like me to go with them."

She thought he was handsome? Given how she had reacted to him at first, that had to be a sign the Scorching was affecting her, affecting her judgment. It was another reason he needed to get her to the *Firebrand*. If there was any way to stop the Scorching from claiming them both, the medical staff on board would know of it. As much as he desired a mate, he couldn't claim her. That was not his mission. "We didn't announce ourselves, and we don't intend to. I'll explain once we're on our way."

She took a single step towards him, then darted away again. "I need my phone. Not that it's working at the moment, but I should still take it. And my purse. Oh, and these!" She returned to the kitchen and grabbed the tin of cookies he had sampled. "I eat when I'm nervous. If I'm doing this, I might as well be prepared." She slipped the tin into her bag and rejoined him, taking his hand with trembling fingers.

He drew her close and activated the teleportation device on his wrist, setting a brief countdown period before it initiated. "I am going to teleport us to my ship. The process is not painful, but it is disorienting and somewhat unpleasant. It won't feel like it, but I will be with you the whole time."

"It's okay. I'm used to being alone."

Her words shredded what was left of his control. "You will never be alone again, *kaheya*." He pulled her into his arms, crushing a kiss to her soft mouth as the world around them disappeared, and they were transported through the void.

3

———

Gwen pinched herself. She had to be dreaming. There was no way this could be real, could it? Men who looked like Kash wouldn't look twice at someone like her, never mind pull her into his arms and kiss her. And holy hotness, the man could kiss. He slanted his mouth across hers in an act of undeniable possession, and she felt the impact all the way down to her toes.

Strong arms held her close, letting her feel the hard planes of his body pressed against her. His lips tasted hers, his beard rough against her skin. She felt a rush of heat that set her blood boiling and made her pussy slick with need. Her head spun like she'd had too much wine and she leaned into Kash, wrapping her arms around his waist to steady herself.

At that moment, a bone-piercing screech erupted around them. He crushed her to him with enough force to make her gasp, and then everything vanished.

She drifted in an infinite stretch of nothingness. She started to panic and then remembered Kash's words. He'd told her she'd never be alone again, that he would be with her. She clung to that promise, trying to imagine that he was still holding her, despite the fact she couldn't feel her own body. She was part of the void, and it was part of her. The only thing that kept the terror at bay was the memory of Kash's last words.

The world came back in a rush. Her senses were overwhelmed with input. Light. Sound. Colour. Touch. She sucked in a breath and pressed herself against the solid comfort of Kash's body. His heart beat hard beneath his ribs, the tempo almost as fast as hers.

"Well, that sucked. Please tell me we don't have to do that again anytime soon." She whispered against his lips, then her eyes flew open as she reconsidered her words. "Wait. I mean the teleportation part. Not the kissing. Kissing good. Teleport bad." Shit. She was babbling again. He was going to think she was an idiot.

Kash chuckled. The low, rumbling sound rolled through her, somehow making her feel better despite the fact he was laughing at her. "You did well. Most first-timers emerge from the transition disoriented and traumatized."

"You said I wouldn't be alone, even if it felt like I was." She leaned her head back to look into his eyes. "I believed you."

A gleam of gold flashed in Kash's eyes, dazzling her. Before she could comment, he speared his fingers into her hair and bowed his head, ravishing her mouth with another kiss. Lips slanted across hers in a full-force sensual attack that had her senses reeling all over again. He nipped her lower lip in silent demand, and she opened her mouth to him, inviting him in. His tongue tangled with hers, a low groan of need rising from his throat.

He guided her backwards a few steps until her back was pressed against a cool, smooth surface. He didn't stop moving until she was pinned in place by his body. The hard line of his cock easily felt against her stomach. His hand left her hair, tracing its way down her shoulder, over her breast, to finally stop at her hip. Without a word, he took hold of her with both hands, lifting her until she was eye to eye with him, her feet dangling far above the floor.

Panic warred with arousal at his quiet display of strength. No one had tried to pick her up since she was a little girl. She was too fat for any man to even try. Now Kash knew exactly how much she weighed. The thought mortified her.

She tore her mouth from his, turning her head to hide her embarrassment. "Stop. Put me down, please."

He froze. "Did I hurt you?"

"No. You'll be the one who ends up hurt if you keep trying to hold me up like this. I'm too heavy to lift."

"Too heavy?" Kash sounded indignant. "I am a soldier of Pyros, not one of the weak males of your species. I could carry you around for several of your days without discomfort."

"You could? You'd want to do that?" It was getting increasingly hard to think. Her thoughts were muddled, her heart was pounding, and all she wanted to do was throw her arms around Kash's neck and kiss him again.

He chuckled, and she felt the sound roll through her like the tolling of a church bell. "Look at me, so that you see the truth of my words."

She turned her head to find him staring at her, his hazel eyes bright with desire and his expression open.

"Having you in my arms is no hardship."

He was telling the truth.

That made her uncomfortable, as did the way he was staring at her. Men didn't look at her that way, like she was a triple chocolate sundae and they were coming off a three-day fast. She decided it was time for a distraction. She finally looked around her, taking in the gleaming walls and strangely empty space they were standing in. "So, uh, where are we right now?"

"We are in the airlock of the shuttle I used to get here. The teleportation device is only good for short distances." Kash gave her a quick kiss and shifted his hold, cradling her in his arms. "And speaking of the shuttle, I should be flying us out of here. I'm not actually authorized to be on the surface."

"You're not supposed to be here? Why not? Your friends are."

They exited the airlock through a door that simply appeared in the wall with a wave of Kash's hand, entering an equally featureless corridor. White walls, pale orange floors, and nothing else but a few discreet keypads set flush with the walls.

"Joran is the crown prince of Pyros, and Vadir is one of the richest, most influential males on my world, and many others besides. Only the elite have been granted permission to undertake this mission."

Gwen stared at him, perplexed. "But, you're perfect. I mean, look at you. Any woman would be thrilled to have you as their match. And who made those stupid rules, anyway? I get why I was rejected, but you?"

"Who rejected you?" He ignored everything but the last thing she'd said.

"Star-Crossed. This interstellar matchmaking service your people cooked up. I applied, too. Lisa and Maggie got accepted, but they didn't want me. And you didn't answer my other questions."

His arms tightened around her. "You ask questions in bunches. How do you even keep track of the answers?"

"That wasn't an answer. That was another question."

His lips curved into a brief smile. "It was."

When he didn't say anything more, she rolled her eyes at him, which made him smile again. She liked it when he did that. She got the feeling Kash didn't smile that often. "So, who decided you couldn't claim a mate or a match or whatever?"

They entered a small cockpit area, with two seats and a console full of monitors and panels marked in a language she'd never seen before. He set her down in one of the chairs, taking the time to fit her with a kind of safety harness before taking the other seat. His fingers flew over the console, activating lights and monitors.

The idea that they were leaving Earth was more than she could deal with, so she trained all her attention on Kash. His words. His actions. The low rumble of his voice. She'd never been turned on by a man's voice before. Not until she'd met him.

Everything about him made her hot. She was a reclusive bookworm who had been known to stammer and flee a room if a man so much as asked her name. Yet, she'd walked out of her house with a smoking hot alien who kissed like a god and told her she was tiny. Either she was losing her mind, or the universe had stopped making sense. Either way, she wasn't in a rush to go back to the way things had been.

"King Janus, the ruler of my planet, was the one who decided who would be selected for matching with human females."

She snorted. "Well, that explains why his son made the list."

"Prince Joran made the list because no prince can ascend to the throne until they are mated, thus ensuring that the family line will continue. Joran's true mate was not on Pyros. The need to find the one female destined for him is the reason we are all here."

"Wait. You're telling me that Maggie is the prince's true mate? How can you tell? And how is that even possible?"

"You are asking your questions in bunches again. I will answer as best I can once we have left the surface. Would you like to watch our ascent?"

"Could I?"

He looked at her askance, his fingers keying in another set of commands. "I would not have offered if it wasn't possible."

The front wall of the cockpit was suddenly filled with lights. The city of Vancouver was stretched out beneath them, glittering like a thousand stars nestled together. The lights ended abruptly at the coastline, and beyond that was nothing but the pitch-black water of the Pacific Ocean.

"It looks so beautiful. I had no idea." She leaned toward the image, trying to memorize every detail.

"Neither did I." Kash wasn't looking at the monitor, though. He was staring straight at her.

He could have left the shuttle's onboard computer to handle the flight back to the *Firebrand*. Normally, Kash would have done exactly that, but there was nothing normal about this trip. He needed to stay busy, with his mind on the flight and his hands on the console. If he didn't, then he'd have Gwen in his arms again before they arrived. After a lifetime of discipline and focus, the Gods had presented him with a temptation he couldn't resist. Gwen.

By the Flames of the First One, she was lovely. He tore his gaze away from her, locking his eyes on the controls.

The memory of how she'd felt nestled in his arms was branded in his mind forever. So was the moment that the Spark had arced between them, announcing to the universe that she was the one he'd given up hope of ever finding. Why did the Gods have to bring her into his life now? He couldn't claim her. He had a mission to fulfill. Lives to protect. And above all that, he was not one of the males selected for matches. To claim her would mean defying a royal command.

"Kash?"

Gwen's soft voice wrapped around him like a physical caress, sending all the blood rushing straight to his cock. As his dick strained against the tight confines of his pants, he wondered why any human male would wear such clothes. He couldn't move, fight, or even react to a female without discomfort. Were they intended to emasculate the males as some form of punishment? He shifted in his chair like a bored recruit, but it didn't help.

"Is it okay if I talk, or am I distracting you?"

"You're not distracting me," he lied.

"You said you'd answer my questions about true mates once we were in the air." She gestured to the view. "We're not on Earth anymore."

He glanced over to her. She had turned her chair to face him, her curiosity overcoming her interest in the fast receding lights of her home. Once again, he was struck by her strength and courage. Even granting that her judgment had likely been compromised by the Scorching, she was still accepting all that he'd told her without panic or fear. Maybe these humans weren't so primitive after all.

"As I understand it, humans can choose to bond and create younglings with anyone they chose. It's different for my people. We cannot procreate with anyone but our true mate. When we find them, we are drawn together and form a bond that lasts for the rest of our lives. It's also the only way for a Pyrosian to unlock their power over flame."

"One person? That's it? Out of an entire world, you all have to find the *one* person that's your match? How is that even possible? What happens if you never find each other?"

He smiled as she hit him with another barrage of questions, even though the answers to her queries were nothing to smile about. "In the past, we had great gatherings. All those who sought their mate would attend, meeting with as many others as they could, hoping to find the one they were destined for. Now, we have databases that can determine likely matches. Once the pair are both adults, that information is sent to them, and they can meet. If the match is true, then they are together for the rest of their lives."

"Sort of like how Star-Crossed works?" she asked, then frowned, her dark eyes turning stormy. "Or is it *exactly* how it works? Did you build a database of Earth girls?"

If she was smart enough to make that leap in logic, there was no point in compounding matters by denying the truth. "We did."

"And then your king sent his son and a handpicked selection of Pyrosian elites to come here and claim human women? Do they even get a say? Will I ever get to see my friends again?"

"We are not barbarians. Any female who was matched has the right to refuse. And yes, I will do my best to ensure that you see your friends again. I give you my word."

"Why are you doing this?"

"Because my people are dying out. Every generation there are fewer females born, and more males live their lives without finding their mate. We had to find another species to reproduce with. Against all odds, we found one. Humans.

"We believed that these pairings would be something less than a true match, but close enough to allow reproduction. In at least two cases, however, the matches have been perfect. Your friends aren't answering you because they are in the thrall of what we call the Scorching. It is the mating fever that begins when a matched pair first touch."

Her shoulders drooped. "So, odds are good they'll be leaving with their true mates when this is done? And since I don't have a match, I can't go with them. I'm glad they get the right to choose, though. That's good. Lisa always wanted to travel. I guess she's going to get to see more than she ever dreamed of. New planets and everything. And they'll be heroes. Helping to save your planet."

"The males they were destined for will give them good lives. Your friend, Maggie, will be a queen one day."

Gwen winced. "Oh man, that's right. She's really not going to love that idea. She always tried to stay out of the spotlight and live quietly. You're sure they're a true match?"

"I'm certain. They experienced the Spark."

Gwen's eyes rounded. "You mean, like the blue spark-thing that happened when we touched?"

Flames and fury. He shouldn't have mentioned the damned Spark.

When he didn't answer her, she stiffened and turned to face forward again. "It *was* that Spark thing you're talking about, wasn't it? But I was rejected from the program, so it must be a glitch. According to your database, I'm not good enough to be your true mate."

"The Gods make the matches, not a computer." He

didn't know what else to say. When he glanced over at Gwen, she was so still and quiet she might have been carved from stone. Shoulders rigid, hands clasped tightly in front of her, her eyes locked on the viewscreen directly ahead.

Seeing her like that and knowing he was the cause of her distress made him physically ache. He wasn't worthy of a mate. He was too scarred and battle-hardened to be a good match for any female. Especially not one as amazing as Gwen. There had to be a way to undo this so she would be free to find someone else. Someone who would treasure her and always put her needs first. She deserved that, and he couldn't give it to her. He had to put his duty to the crown first. Always.

The silence between them continued for the rest of the journey. The only words spoken were from the ship's computer, and the only sound was the rhythmic drumming of his fingers on the edge of the console.

Once they docked, he unfastened his harness and turned to assist Gwen with hers, only to discover she had managed to undo herself and was already out of her chair and backed into a corner of the cockpit.

"Now what happens?" Her words were clipped, her hands still clenched in front of her. It wasn't until he looked carefully that he saw that she held them that way to hide their trembling. She was afraid. Whatever trust she'd had in him was gone.

"Now, we leave the ship. First, we'll go to the airlock again, and stay in there a few minutes during decontamination. Then I'm taking you to medical to have your burns attended to."

"You're going to fix my hand?"

"You are injured. We can heal that in a matter of seconds. Why would I not do that for you?"

"Because I'm a problem you need to deal with, not a guest. I realize that, now. I was stupid not to see it before. I'm a risk. You didn't come to tell me about Maggie and Lisa out of the goodness of your heart. You weren't supposed to come to the planet at all. You said so yourself. You had to come because I know too much and I was about to call the police about my missing friends." Her brow furrowed. "Did you do something to my phone? Is that why I couldn't call anyone the last time I tried?"

"Yes, we blocked your communications. I'll explain the rest once we're in the airlock."

He exited the cockpit and let her fall in behind him. He wanted to touch her, to take her hand, but he didn't. It would only accelerate the Scorching.

They re-entered the empty space of the airlock, he activated the decontamination program, and turned to face Gwen. "You are more than a problem to be dealt with, Gwen Hudson. You are a guest on this ship, not a prisoner. No harm will come to you, I swear. I should warn you, that while most of the crew have been giving rudimentary training in your language, not all of them will be fluent. There may be miscommunications."

"So, that's not some nifty translator device you're

using to speak with me? You actually learned English? How long did that take? And what's with the blue lights?"

"The light is part of the decontamination process. And yes, I learned your language. We were all given cognitive augmentation containing information on language and customs. The uploads were done while I slept." He'd take her rapid-fire questions over unhappy silence any time. At least they were talking again.

"You learned English in your *sleep*?" she sighed. "I wish we had that tech. I could take a nap, wake up, and be able to read books in a new language. I can speak and read a little French, but most of what I know comes from reading the French side of my box of Corn Flakes."

The airlock lights strobed green, and the outer door opened, revealing the open space of the shuttle deck.

"Medical is this way. Follow me."

A few uniformed crewmen worked on the vessels, and all of them turned to stare as Gwen stepped into view. She was the first human they'd seen in the flesh, and all of them were curious.

Gwen hunched her shoulders and dropped her gaze to the floor. "Why are they staring?"

Kash raised his voice and added a booming tone of authority to his words. "They're staring because they've forgotten their manners. Get back to your duties, or your next mission assignments will be guarding grain shipments to the Qualla mining colonies against *paka* infestations." He then repeated the entire statement in Pyrosian, and by the time he was done, there wasn't an idle crew member in sight.

Good. No one stares at my mate but me.

He banished the errant thought and headed for the medical bay. He needed to be thinking clearly, and that wasn't going to happen while he was in the thrall of the Scorching. It was time to put an end to this madness before it consumed him completely.

4

When Kash started barking orders in his strange, sharp-toned language, she gave up trying to pretend everything was normal. The reality of her situation came back in a rush, swamping her in doubts and making her question her sanity. She'd let herself be taken away from her planet by an alien. God, she'd even kissed him!

Worse, she wanted to kiss him again.

Every growly, grumpy syllable he uttered made her heart race and filled her with needs so intense it hurt not to reach out and touch him. The only thing that made her ache worse was knowing that he didn't want her. Or maybe he did, since he'd kissed her, but he didn't want to want her. Why else wouldn't he have told her she was his mate?

She followed Kash out of the hangar and down a brightly lit corridor. The floors were a pale yellow, and the walls had a hint of orange to them. Every few meters, panels were set into the walls, and she recognized them as being similar to the one Kash had used to open the door to the airlock.

They passed several crew members along the way, all wearing military-style uniforms of black and orange, and everyone greeted Kash with a hand-to-heart type of salute as they went by. Both the men and women were tall and fit. They looked surprisingly human, with similar hair colour and features, though they all seemed to have varying shades of golden skin instead of the wildly varied hues of humans, and she noticed that some of them had golden eyes.

"In here." Kash stopped outside another panel. A portion of the wall vanished, and she was ushered inside.

Apart from the beds, it didn't look like any hospital she'd ever been in. She breathed a soft sigh of relief. Hospitals were far from her favourite places. The sharp, medicinal odours and hushed sounds reminded her of the family members she'd lost.

Her mother had battled her cancer for three years before it finally killed her. Gwen had spent so much time in hospitals, she'd actually taken her first steps in a cancer ward. Her Gran had spent the last few days of her life in a hospital bed, too. The stroke stole her ability to move and to speak, but Gwen had stayed with her until the end.

That was when the nurses had discovered that the

little girl haunting their halls had lied about having anyone to take care of her. The next day, with only a bag of clothes and a handful of treasures she'd managed to sneak into her things, Gwen was placed in the system and sent off to a foster home.

"This is a hospital? Where's the equipment? The patients?" She gestured around at the empty beds and comfortable surroundings. The walls were a warmer shade of yellow in here, the lighting was soft and soothing, and the air was clean of any scent at all.

A tall, blonde man walked into view, his brows raising in surprise as he spotted her. "Human?" She recognized the first word he spoke, but the rest of his comments were in the same language Kash had uttered while they were in the hangar.

He and Kash spoke for a bit, and she got the impression that Kash wasn't happy about whatever he was being told. She was also fairly certain that she was the topic under discussion since she heard her name mentioned more than once.

Eventually, she got tired of being talked about and interjected. "It's not polite to talk about someone when they can't understand what you're saying."

The blond gave her an apologetic smile. "I am sorry. You are correct, this does concern you. My name is Torel, and I am what you would call a doctor. Would you show me your burns? The Commander would like me to treat them for you."

She held out her hand, palm up. "It's really nothing. They'll be gone in a few days."

"She treated them with water and plant sap, Torel. I trust we can do better for our guest."

"It's aloe vera gel, and it's very good for burns. It's the best we primitives can manage, Commander."

The doctor carefully inspected her burns, his touch gentle. "And I'm sure it works very well. My mother has an herbal remedy for respiratory ailments that's as effective as anything ever synthesized on my world. However, we have developed some very effective technology for regenerating injured tissue. I can have this healed in a matter of moments if you will allow it?"

"I'm not Pyrosian, though. Will it work on me?"

He nodded. "All lifeforms are similar at the cellular level. It will work. You won't even feel it."

"Then you have my permission." The doctor kept hold of her hand and led her to a simple white table with a single chair beside it. "Sit there, and place your hand on the surface with the injured side facing up." He moved her hand into position.

She looked at the ordinary table with some doubt but followed directions. "Now what?"

Kash loomed over the table, arms folded over his massive chest, and scowl on his face. "Now Torel lets go of you before he's the one who needs treatment."

"That's the second time you've threatened someone since we got here. That's some leadership style you've got, Commander."

"Torel knows better."

The blond chuckled. "He's not normally quite this...I think the word is grumpy. He's having a most difficult day."

Kash growled something in Pyrosian, and the low, guttural tone sent a surge of lust coursing through her. Her nipples tightened, her clit began to swell, and heat flowed over her as if she'd been dipped in molten honey.

The doctor glanced up at her, and she could read the concern in his expression. "Are you feeling heated? A sudden rise in your body temperature?"

"Yes." That much she could admit to without embarrassing herself.

Torel looked past her to Kash and said something to him in Pyrosian. Kash shook his head, and the two argued for several seconds before Kash finally barked out a single word and stalked away.

"Why is he so angry with me?" She asked, pitching her voice to a mere whisper.

"It's not you he's angry with. He'll explain once I'm done here." Torel waved his hand over a corner of the tabletop, and a keypad appeared out of nowhere. He typed in a few characters, and gave her a reassuring smile. "You're going to see a golden glow appear around your hand. Try not to move until it dissipates. It won't take long."

"Okay." She tried to ignore Kash's brooding presence as he watched her from the far side of the room.

Instead, she kept her eyes and her attention focused on her hand. The glow appeared exactly as Torel said it would. She couldn't feel anything, but as she watched, the redness faded, the blisters grew smaller and then vanished as if they'd never been there at all. In a matter of seconds, it was over, and she lifted her hand to stare at it in amazement.

"You're fully healed. If you feel any tingling or itching in the next few hours, have the Commander contact me." Torel looked over at Kash. "She's all yours, Commander."

"Apparently." Kash didn't sound at all pleased about it, either. "Come with me, Gwen. There are matters we need to discuss."

Torel lowered his voice again. "Disregard his temper. The Commander is not used to being told no. That's all."

He walked away before she could ask Torel what he meant.

"Gwen Hudson, you need to come with me. Now."

"You might be a Commander, but you're not my boss. I don't answer to you."

"*Kaheya*. Please." He held out his hand to her.

She joined him, but instead of taking his hand, she passed him her bag, weighed down by the tin of cookies she'd stuffed inside. "Where to, now?"

"My quarters."

Why would he want her in his quarters? "Lead the way."

Kash felt like he'd been sideswiped by a comet. His life was spinning out of control, and every time he got close to stabilizing things, something happened and it all went up in flames again. He had convinced himself that Torel would be able to stop the onset of the Scorching, and things could return to normal.

Torel had sent that hope crashing into the heart of the nearest star. There was no known way to stop the Scorching. The mating fever was irreversible. Resisting it would only cause pain and possible madness. He'd been willing to accept that risk for himself, but Torel had noticed Gwen's symptoms. If they didn't give in to the Scorching, she would suffer, too.

The Gods were playing games with him. They'd given him the one thing he'd always wanted, but to claim it, he'd have to forsake duty and defy his king.

He strode through the ship, driven to haste by the needs of the Scorching. He was so caught up in his thoughts, several minutes passed before he realized that Gwen was struggling to maintain his pace. Her legs were far shorter than his, forcing her to jog to keep up.

He stopped, pivoted, and scooped her in his arms without a word.

"Hey! What are you doing? You can't carry me."

"Are you questioning my strength again? Have I not made it clear that I am more than able to support your weight? You are small. Your legs are shorter than mine. This way will be faster."

"You're at least a foot taller than I am, but that doesn't mean I'm small. I'm five-foot-four. Maybe you're just too big. Did that ever occur to you? You could have slowed down a little. Why the sudden hurry to be alone with me? The last time we were alone, you said I was a mistake. That being matched to you was some kind of glitch."

Anger, regret, and desire blended together into a maelstrom that threatened to snap the last shreds of his control. "No. *You* said you were a glitch. I said that matches were made by the Gods."

"What's the difference? God, Gods, or computer. Someone made a mistake. You don't want me."

He cradled her against him and broke into a jog. "You're about to learn how wrong you are about that, *kaheya*. Wanting you was never the problem."

"Then what is your problem, you big jerk? Because so help me, if you kiss me and then reject me again, I'm going to—to—" She waved her hand in the air between them. "I'll do something, and you won't like it."

He laughed. The entire crew of this star cruiser obeyed his orders without question. Grown males would go out of their way to avoid causing him displeasure. His scars caused unease and distress to any who looked on him. The only being in the galaxy who wasn't afraid of him was the small, furious female in his arms.

She huffed at him and poked a finger into his chest. "Don't you dare laugh at me! I've had a miserable day. I lost my job, got told I'm too old to date, found out the two people I care about will be leaving me to go live on another planet, and now the hottest man I've ever met can't decide what he really wants."

"We'll discuss this once we've reached my quarters. This is not a conversation you want to have in public."

She lapsed into silence. Crewmen gawked at them as he jogged past but he ignored them. For the first time in his life, he didn't care what others thought.

They finally reached his quarters, a door appearing automatically after reading his biometrics and confirming his identity. No one else could leave or enter this room without his express permission.

The second the door sealed them in, Gwen twisted in his arms. "You can let me go now."

"No. I'm never letting you go. I can't." He set her back on her feet, then walked her backwards until she was pressed between him and the nearest wall.

"You said..."

"Forget what we said before, and listen to me now. The Spark between us heralded the beginning of the Scorching. I thought that if I brought you here, Torel would be able to administer something to stop its progression. You'd be able to make your own choice. I'd be able to obey the orders I was given."

She tipped her head back to stare up at him. "You asked him to undo this thing between us?"

"I did."

"That's what you were arguing about. You wanted to be free of me, and he told you it wasn't going to happen."

"I wanted you to have a choice."

She frowned. "If you meant that, you'd have asked me if I wanted to be matched with you. You didn't. This wasn't about my choices. It was about yours."

He wanted to argue with her, to tell her she was wrong, but the truth was, she might be right. At least in part. And now wasn't the time for anger. They'd have a lifetime for blame, recriminations, and regrets. "Maybe. But that doesn't matter anymore."

"Why not?" She leaned into him, wetting her lower lip with the tip of her tongue. Desire glowed in depths of her eyes, betraying her need for him.

He cupped her soft cheek in his hand, stroking his thumb over her mouth. "Because there's no cure for the Scorching. We're going to be bound together for the rest of our lives, starting now."

She opened her mouth to continue their argument, and he stopped her words with a kiss. The time for words had passed.

Heat streaked through him, leaving trails of desire blazing in its wake. He had tried to convince himself this wasn't real. That he could live without her. One taste of her lips and he knew he'd been lying to himself. She tasted sweet and decadent, like the cookies she'd offered him back in her residence. She was temptation made flesh, and he'd reached the end of his resistance.

She uttered a soft little moan that made his cock turn to stone in a heartbeat. His fingers moved from her cheek to her hair, tangling themselves in her curls. He tugged her head back, and she rose on her toes to kiss him back as she opened her mouth to his.

His tongue danced with hers, hearts racing, mouths mated until there was no breath in his lungs and he felt as if he'd been dipped in a pool of rocket fuel and set on fire.

"Tell me you want this. That you accept me as your mate."

"Promise me that when this Scorching thing ends, you won't blame me for what happened," she retorted.

He gave her the only answer he could, by uttering the words of a vow he never believed he'd make. ""I vow by the Flames of the First One, to protect and cherish my mate—you, Gwen Hudson of Earth. You will be my lover and my beloved companion, every day, from now until we return to the Flame that gave us life. And I will never blame you for coming into my life."

"I believe you." She reached up to caress the scarred side of his face, tracing the wound across his cheek and into the thin line of white hairs that marked its path. "I accept you as my mate. You are handsome, kinder than you pretend to be, and I believe you're a good man--male, even when you're being a grumpy ass. So yes, I want this."

An unfamiliar sense of lightness overcame him, and he burst out laughing. "You must be my true mate. No one else would dare to say such things to me."

"You're even sexier when you smile. You should do that more often. On second thought, maybe not. I only just found you. If you start smiling, I might have to fight to keep you. I've seen the women on this ship. They're gorgeous, and they all look like they could kick my pudgy butt."

"Did I not just promise to protect you? No one will kick you, or harm you in any way. There will be no other females, my *kaheya*. Once we have mated, I will desire no one but you for the rest of my life."

"And how will they know that? Do we wear rings? Matching hats?"

"My eyes will change to gold, and I will gain the ability to summon and manipulate flames. It is a power the Gods only grant to us once we are mated. No one will doubt my status."

She smiled. "Then I vote we get onto the mating bit. It's getting difficult to think. All I want to do is..." she stopped talking and bit her lower lip.

A surge of lust washed over him. "Tell me what you want, *kaheya*."

"You. I want you. I can't believe I'm saying this. I want you naked. With me. Touching me. Kissing me. Anything. God, I want everything."

"That, I can do." He pressed her against the wall with his hips, his lips on hers as he tore off every shred of her clothing. His own clothes took longer, the tight-fitting fabric resisting all attempts to remove it by force. Frustrated, he finally released her.

"Let me help."

Kash groaned aloud as Gwen sank to her knees in front of him, her soft hands removing the garment far faster than he could have.

When his legs were bared, she wrapped both hands around his cock, stroking it from base to tip. Her touch sent him into high orbit. There would be a time for slow, leisurely touches and exploration, but it wasn't going to be now. He needed her too badly to take things slow.

He caught her hands and drew her back to her feet, then lifted her into the air carried her to his bed.

"But I wasn't done with you."

"The Scorching lasts for two of your days. We'll do that later." He settled her gently in the center of the mattress then stood there, staring at her. She was breathtaking. Soft. With generous curves that reflected her kind and compassionate heart.

"Two days? How? I mean, don't you have a ship to run? A mission?"

"It's against procedure for me to retain full command while in the thrall of the Scorching. For the next two days, my only mission is you." Torel had made it clear that if Kash didn't hand over command voluntarily, he'd file the reports to make it happen anyway. It was something else they had argued about while Gwen was being treated. He'd sent a message to his second in command before they'd left the medical bay. While Kash was still nominally in charge, he was not expected on the bridge until the Scorching had passed and his judgment was no longer compromised. Not unless there was an emergency the others couldn't deal with.

The light in her eyes dimmed a little. "I cost you your command?"

"You didn't cost me anything." He'd hurt her again. He joined her on the bed, consumed by the need to hold her and reassure her that this was not her fault. If anyone was to blame, it was the Gods, and they didn't answer to their creations.

He nuzzled a soft point beneath her ear and whispered a piece of advice he'd been given more than once in his life. "Stop thinking so much and let go, little one."

She smiled a little. "I will if you will."

"Agreed." He ran the tip of his tongue over her skin, needing to taste her.

She turned her head so that her lips were next to his ear and whispered. "I ache, Kash. Make the hurting stop."

That, he could do.

He blazed a trail of open-mouthed kisses along her throat and down to her collarbone. She swept a hand over his hair, and that simple contact made his entire body hum.

"You're so beautiful."

"That's the Scorching talking. Are you sure you'll feel the same once it passes?"

"I will feel this way about you for the rest of my life. That isn't going to change."

"You're sure?"

Her lack of confidence made him wonder who had convinced her that she wasn't worthy of such compliments. Someone had lied to her because she was more than worthy.

He cupped one of her breasts in his hands, her nipple tightening as he brushed his thumb over it. "You're still thinking too much." He caught the tight nub of her nipple between his fingers and pinched it lightly. She gasped, and he did it again, determined to bring her into the moment with him.

She shifted to her back, coaxing him to come with her until they were both sprawled across the bed, lips mated in a heated kiss. She coiled one leg around his thigh and rocked into him in silent encouragement. They didn't need words any longer.

He nipped at her lower lip, released it to kiss his way down her body, stopping to nibble and suck at her breasts until her moans filled the air. He drew one pert nipple into his mouth and was rewarded with a keening cry of need.

"Again." Her breathless plea nearly broke him, and

he groaned her name against her skin as he suckled, his thumb and forefinger echoing his actions with her other breast. She arched beneath him, offering him her body, and her actions sent his libido into overdrive. His cock throbbed, thicker and heavier than he'd ever been before. He needed to be inside her, soon. He had to make her his forever, no matter what the cost.

5

———

The Gods of Pyros had gifted her with a god of her own.

Gwen couldn't stop touching him. He was built like a warrior out of legend, all power and grace. His muscle and sinew flowed beneath his golden skin, skin that was marked by scars, mostly faded now. She thought they were sexy. Proof that he was a survivor, strong enough to withstand whatever life had thrown at him. She tended to hide in her books and daydreams when things got hard, but Kash hadn't hidden. He'd fought back.

He kissed his way down her body, laying claim to every inch of her as his calloused hands explored every curve. Usually, she preferred to make love in the dark so that she wasn't embarrassed, but with Kash, things were different. She knew he wanted her. And while she wasn't convinced that desire wouldn't fade away eventually, for now, she trusted that his desire was as real as hers was for him.

The taste of him was still in her mouth, a subtle, spicy flavour that blended with the growing scent of arousal and need that filled the air around them. She ran her hands through his hair, loving the way it felt against the palms of her hands. He worked his way lower, and she uncoiled her leg from around his, letting her thighs fall open. He moved between her parted legs, his mouth like a brand against her skin, the rasp of his beard over her belly an erotic sensation she'd never known before.

"You're a feast for the senses," he murmured, and lowered his head to brush his lips over her inner thigh. Her breath caught in her throat and she went still, anticipating where his next touch would be. His hands stroked up her thighs slowly, until his fingers brushed her outer lips. He parted her folds, blowing a puff of warm breath across her clitoris.

"This will give you pleasure, yes?" He asked, then swiped his tongue across her clit.

"Yes!" She nearly screamed the word as ecstasy flowed through her.

He did it again and again, pushing her relentlessly towards release. She arched off the bed, her hips pumping, grinding her pussy against the exquisite torture of his mouth.

"Kash!" she cried his name as he pressed deeper, his

tongue lashing at her clit before sucking the tender flesh into his mouth. That made her moan aloud with need. He growled in encouragement, the vibrations adding another layer of pleasure to the onslaught. He slid a thick finger into her channel, and the wave she'd been riding finally crested and broke. Her world shattered as she hurtled into an orgasm so intense that the world around her vanished, leaving her adrift in a sea of bliss.

It was his kiss that brought her back to her senses, his lips tasting of both of them as he kissed her with tender passion.

"Are you ready to be mine, *kaheya*?"

She twined her arms around his neck and nodded. "I am."

"Thank the Gods. I'm on fire to have you." He kissed her again as he settled his body into the cradle of her thighs, his impressive cock pressed against the seam of her pussy.

"You're mine." He arched his back and slid inside her, moving slowly to give her time to adjust. He was big enough to hurt her, but he didn't. He claimed her an inch at a time, even though his body shook with need and his eyes flashed from hazel to gold and back again.

He didn't stop until he was fully sheathed inside her. She was fuller than she'd ever been. Deliciously so. As their bodies touched, she moved her hips and gasped as a wave of pleasure washed through her.

She moaned and sank her nails into his shoulders, urging him to move.

He growled, the primitive sound turning her on even more. He lowered his head to kiss her, then settled his hands on the bed and pushed himself up, freeing his hips to move. Slowly at first, every stroke going so deep she was pinned to the mattress. Each time he withdrew, she followed, not wanting to lose their connection.

Their bodies shifted as they found their rhythm, his cock angling to slide along her clit at the beginning of each thrust, her legs wrapping around his waist to bring them closer together.

"More," she whispered the single word, barely able to believe she could be so bold.

"I'll give you everything."

His words filling her heart with hope. His next kiss was hot and hungry, scorching her lips with the heat of his passion. His tongue speared into her mouth as he drove his cock deep into her body.

A scream of pleasure rose from her throat and the two of them came together in an explosion of fiery need. His eyes flared a brilliant gold, his expression one of pure rapture as he orgasmed with a bellow that echoed off the walls of his quarters.

As he came, his cock thickened and swelled, pressing against her most sensitive spots and sending her into another orgasm of her own. Her inner walls flexed around him, milking him of every drop.

Breathless and trembling with the aftershocks of her release, she was still struggling to think clearly when Kash nuzzled her cheek. "The swelling will subside soon, but until then, we're locked together. Try not to move too much."

"I don't think I could move if my life depended on it."

His head jerked up. "Did I injure you?"

"No...oh wow. Your eyes. They really are gold now."

He stared at her, those newly minted eyes wide with shock. "As are yours."

"What? How? That's...that's not supposed to happen, is it?"

"Calm, *kaheya*. No moving, remember?"

"If you want me to stay still, then don't tell me my eyes changed colours." She forced herself to relax and take a breath, then another.

"It was a surprise to me, as well. You are even more beautiful this way." He grinned, looking downright smug. "And now everyone will know you are claimed."

"I still don't understand how this is possible. I didn't even feel anything."

"Allow me to check something." Kash raised his head. "Computer. Scan the Star-Crossed files for Gwen Hudson's information. Confirm presence of Pyrosian genes."

"Checking."

Gwen stayed quiet, too stunned to speak. She might have alien DNA? Why hadn't anyone mentioned that? And how the hell was that even possible? And when did they get her DNA?

"Confirmed. File indicates subject Gwen Hudson positive for Pyrosian genetic markers."

"And they rejected you anyway." Kash shook his head. "How many potential matches did they dismiss? The King needs to know about this before the next mission."

"What are you talking about? I'm human. You said so yourself."

"Apparently not. Well, not completely. We found traces of our genome scattered throughout your population. It's why we're here. Those traces prove that our races are compatible for reproduction. No one expected this, though." He caressed her cheek, then gently withdrew from her body and settled down at her side.

"How? What does this mean? Can I see?" She wasn't sure how she felt about being part alien. Would this make it easier for her to be accepted as Kash's mate?

"Computer. Set the wall behind the bed to reflection mode."

"Affirmative."

"Now you can see for yourself." Kash rose to one elbow and gestured behind him.

She sat up and turned to look, gasping as she caught sight of her reflection. The change was shocking. "This makes it easier to believe I'm part alien. How is this possible?"

"We're not sure. The best theory is that ages ago when we were actively colonizing other worlds, one of our colony ships must have made its way to your planet. There's no record of that happening, but there were ships that set out and were never heard from again."

"This is going to take some time to get used to."

"Do you not like the change? Do my eyes bother you?"

"Your eyes are gorgeous. Just like the rest of you. But you knew this would happen to you. I got up this morning thinking this was going to be another ordinary day." She laughed and threw out her arms to take in everything around them. "I'm on a spaceship orbiting Earth, and apparently my soulmate is an alien. Oh, and let's not forget that my friends have also been claimed by aliens, all because Lisa talked us into signing up for an online dating service months ago."

"I shall have to thank your friend Lisa when I meet her." He stroked a possessive hand along her thigh.

"Me too." She looked around, taking her first real look at Kash's quarters. There wasn't much to see. The furniture was all made from the same off-white material that looked something like plastic, while the cushions and bed linens were all patterned after the uniforms she'd seen the crew wearing: black, with hints of orange and white. The only thing out of place were their clothes, which were still strewn in heaps across the floor.

It wasn't anything like she'd imagined a starship would look like, but if she had any doubts about where she was, and who she was with, all she had to do was look in a mirror.

———

Kash knew that his rooms were barren and cold compared to the comfortable haven Gwen had created for herself back on Earth. He could claim that it was because these were only temporary quarters, but his residence back on Pyros wasn't much better. A lifetime of military service had made him a minimalist. He could live in the palace, but he'd always chosen to reside near his men. Now that Gwen was part of his life, that would have to change. Flames. Everything was going to change, now. He stared in wonder at the female curled against his side. He was a mated male.

Curious, he held up his hand and focused his thoughts, visualizing flames enveloping his fingers. The fire erupted almost instantly.

"Whoa! Warn a girl, would you?" Gwen flinched, then retreated from the flames.

"Apologies. I hadn't expected it to work the first time I tried it." He banished the flames with a flick of his hand.

"Isn't fire a bad thing in space? What happens if

you set the room on fire? Or me, for that matter? I've already been burned once today, thank you."

"As my mate, you are immune to my flames. And given what we are, every ship in the fleet is outfitted with extensive fire prevention measures. There was a time when there were enough mated soldiers that they could work together to form a sort of living weapon. We were feared throughout worlds, and none dared to threaten us." He summoned the flame again, a tiny blaze that danced on his outstretched palm.

"You're sure I won't get burned?"

"I would never risk harming you, *kaheya*."

She ran her fingers up the length of his forearm, pausing when she reached his hand. "I don't feel much heat."

"Nor do I."

It pleased him that she trusted him enough to test the flame, passing her hand over of it, and then through it.

"That's amazing. I thought you were a badass before. Now, you're like a badass dual-class fighter wizard."

"A what?" He had no idea what a wizard was, but he liked the sound of it.

"I guess your education didn't include Tolkien's books or Dungeons and Dragons. A wizard is someone who can wield magic. Not that magic really exists. Well, maybe it does. I mean, Lisa drew a picture of Vadir weeks ago, and she got every detail right. So maybe?" She closed her eyes. "I'm too tired to deal with that possibility right now. I'm still dealing with the fact aliens are real."

"You can tell me more about wizards and Tolkien another time. And I would like to hear about dragons, too. The Romaki dragon clans will likely be very interested to hear that there is a word for their species on your planet. Perhaps the Pyrosians were not the only ones to visit your world."

"Wait. What? There are space dragons? Big, fire-breathing lizard things with wings and piles of treasure?"

"There are two Romaki clans: Snow and Fire. They are an ancient race, and yes, in their beast forms they do have wings." He chuckled. "And Vadir would tell you that they enjoy holding onto their wealth. He was part of the last round of trade negotiations between our races, and it did not end well."

Gwen snuggled in beside him with a sleepy groan. "Lisa is going to be so, so, smug. Not only do aliens exist, but dragons do, too."

"You should rest while you can. Neither of us have slept much, yet, and we're both going to be at the mercy of the Scorching for the next while." He reached over and drew the top blanket over them both.

She draped her arm across his stomach and settled her head on his chest. "You'll be here when I wake up, right?"

"I'll be here, *kaheya*." He had nowhere else to be.

For the first time in years, he had no duties to perform or plan for. No responsibilities to fulfill. It felt wrong, somehow.

"Good," she murmured. There was a short pause, then she said, "I'm glad you disobeyed orders tonight. I can't imagine how this night would have gone if you hadn't come for me."

"Me, either."

She fell into an exhausted sleep within minutes, trusting him to watch over her as she slept. His little mate had given him so many gifts. Unsurpassed pleasure, acceptance, and now, her trust. He wasn't worthy of her. She deserved someone without his scars. Someone like Vadir or the prince. She deserved more than him, but now that he had claimed her, he could never let her go.

An hour passed, but he couldn't sleep. There was too much in his head, and in his heart. When should he inform his liege that he'd taken a mate against orders? Would he be punished? It was possible. So long as they did not blame Gwen, he'd accept any punishment. His family would want to know of his good fortune. His mother and father would be happy, and Kylara, his sister, would be ecstatic to learn she had a mate-sister at long last.

He was still sorting through his thoughts when a soft chime sounded, and a red light flashed on the wall monitor nearest the bed. Not wanting to wake Gwen, he rose and activated another monitor, far enough away that he could speak without disturbing her. He didn't bother dressing first. If they were contacting him now, they'd have good reason. Whatever it was, he doubted it was good news.

His second in command, Bortan Zell, snapped off a quick salute as he appeared on the monitor. "Commander, we have a situation."

"Report."

"Vadir Rahal missed his last check-in. There's no reply to our messages, and the *Redshift 7* is not showing on our scans."

His gut knotted. "He was supposed to keep a passive beacon active so we'd be able to track his ship even when shielded. What happened?"

Zell stiffened. "We're still investigating, sir. It appears there was a communication breakdown during shift change. The incoming officer was not aware they were supposed to be tracking a secondary beacon."

"How long ago did we lose contact?" Kash asked through gritted teeth.

"Last contact with *Redshift 7* was six hours ago. Because the beacon was passive, the ship's systems were not automatically tracking it, so we can't be certain—"

Kash cut him off. "Find a way to become certain, and find it before I get to the bridge. Denza out."

The monitor went black, and so did his mood. This was what happened when he forfeited his responsibilities for even a few hours. The lives of two males were in his hands, and he'd allowed himself to be distracted. That couldn't happen again.

Guilt and anger churned inside him as he donned his uniform and made himself presentable in short order. He was almost at the door when he stopped and turned around to look at Gwen. She was fast asleep, curled in his bed with one arm thrown over his pillow. She'd sleep for another two hours at least. More than enough time to find out what had happened and get back to her before she woke.

6

Gwen woke with a gasp, her heart pounding.

Why do I always wake up before the good bit?" She groggily recalled the erotic dream she'd had. She'd been with the sexiest man she'd ever seen, dark and serious, with the most amazing golden eyes. The details had been so vivid, the whole dream so realistic, that even awake she was still shaking with need and out of breath.

She sat up, groaning as her muscles protested the sudden movement. She ached like she had gone to the gym and tried to make up for six months of inactivity in a single session. She felt overheated, too. Did she have a fever? Gwen reached up to touch the back of her hand to her forehead, then froze as she finally registered her surroundings. She wasn't in her bed, and this was not her room or even her house.

Panic spurred her sleep-muddled mind, and the

recollections of the night's events came rushing back. Kash. Spaceships and golden lights. Kash naked. *Whoa.* She flopped back on the bed. She was on a spaceship in orbit around Earth, and her dream lover wasn't a dream at all.

"Kash?"

No answer. He wouldn't have left her alone. He'd promised not to. She looked around the room. Their clothes were still in a tangled heap on the floor, along with her purse. Everything was the same as when she'd gone to sleep, but there was no sign of Kash. She called his name again and got out of bed. Feeling vulnerable, she grabbed her shirt off the floor and put it on. That was a mistake. She was so sensitive that even the light touch of the fabric felt like a sensual caress against her skin.

A rush of raw need slammed into her with dizzying force, and she flung out a hand to steady herself against the nearest wall. What the hell was wrong with her? She touched the back of her hand to her forehead and winced. She was burning up. She staggered around the room, keeping one hand on the wall as she explored. She found a panel and waved her hand over it. A wall slid open, revealing a closet inside. There were a few uniforms that looked like the ones the other crew of the ship wore, and a pair of polished boots sat on the floor. There was space for another pair of boots, and one of the hangers was empty. She already knew he'd left, but seeing the proof of it tore into her like a jagged blade.

He'd broken his promise to stay with her. How could she trust him not to break them all? Did he mean anything he'd said, or was he just trying to keep her quiet and out of the way until he decided what to do with her?

Hurting and unsteady, she went back to her pile of clothing and got dressed. She didn't even bother to try putting on her bra. Just the shirt and pants were torture enough. She was drugged with desire, her body trembling with need for the man who had lied and left her.

"Computer?" She called out to the empty air. "Ship?" She tried again, hoping that some sort of AI would respond to her queries. Nothing happened, and she gave up trying. "Apparently, in space, no one can hear me...at all. Dammit, Kash. Where are you?"

For a brief second, she felt like he was there with her. It was so real she could swear she heard him speak her name. The feeling faded but didn't completely disappear. It was like a whisper in the back of her mind. If Lisa were here, she'd know what to do. Lisa was the one who believed in soulmates, magic, and telepathy. Gwen just read about them.

She looked around again and laughed at herself. She had proof that aliens were real. Maybe the rest of it was, too. Closing her eyes, she tried to focus on the whisper in the back of her mind. The one that felt like Kash. His presence was like a beacon that got brighter the more she focused. She was certain she could find him. They were connected. The bond between them was getting stronger, just as he said it would. How could he leave her alone to deal with all of this by herself?

Hurt, angry, and still drunk on desires she couldn't control, she took a deep breath and made her way over to the panel she hoped would open the door they'd come in by. She waved her hand over it, but no door appeared.

"Come on. I got the damned closet door to open. Why won't you?" She tried poking a few of the buttons, then pressed her palm to the pad. It flashed an ugly shade of orange, and an automated voice uttered a few terse words in Pyrosian.

She tried again, and again the automated voice barked at her. Frustrated, she slammed her hand down on the pad. "Let me out of here!"

Something inside her snapped, and all her fear, hurt, and stress of the past twenty-four hours erupted. She threw back her head and screamed. A roaring filled her ears, drowning out the sound of her voice, and then everything went red.

Kash stared at the forward monitor as if he could command Vadir's beacon to appear on it by force of will alone. There was no sign of the ship, and all their attempts to contact Vadir or the AI that controlled the *Redshift 7* had met with nothing but silence. The crew was working frantically to uncover any trace of the missing vessel. So far, the only fact they'd uncovered was that the ship had powered up its engines and taken off, but they'd vanished shortly thereafter.

The only good news was what they hadn't found. There was no sign of wreckage, and none of the human agencies they were scanning had mentioned anything of concern. It was likely that Vadir's ship had crashed, but they had to be at least semi-operational, or they wouldn't be able to shield themselves from detection.

He needed to find Vadir and get this mission back on a stable orbit. Then, he'd give in to the need that tore through him like a living flame. He knew now why it was called the Scorching. It hurt to be away from Gwen. It was agonizing to deny himself the pleasure of her touch. He embraced the pain. This was his punishment for allowing himself to be distracted. If he'd been on the bridge, the miscommunication would have never happened. But he hadn't been there. He'd handed off the responsibility to others. He'd failed.

"Status update," he demanded.

"Nothing to report, sir."

They were performing a methodical search of the area, but the odds of finding something while the ship was shielded were minimal at best. It beat doing nothing, however. When he had to make his report, he'd be able to say that they'd done everything they could. It wouldn't count for much, though. Not unless they found the ship and got it and its occupants, off the planet before they were detected.

He drummed his fingers against his thigh as he pondered which he dreaded more, telling the king he'd blown the mission, or telling Gwen that her friend Lisa was missing.

Gwen. She'd be awake soon. She was human, so the Scorching shouldn't be affecting her as strongly as it did him, but he'd have to return to her soon. How long had he been away from her? He wasn't sure.

A pang of guilt hit him. He was failing her, too. No matter what he did, it wasn't enough. If Torel learned he was back on the bridge, he'd put him on report. If he left, then the search for Vadir could go awry. If he stayed, then Gwen would wake alone. He was damned no matter what course he plotted.

Another flare of red-hot need speared through him, and this time, he heard an echo of someone else's pain. *Gwen*. She was awake, alone, and hurting. He'd broken his promise. That knowledge spurred him to make the choice he probably should have made from the beginning. He turned on his heel and headed for the door.

"You have the bridge."

Three steps from the exit, a klaxon sounded, accompanied by the voice of the ship's computer. "Fire in Section 09-1. Repeat. Fire in Section 09-1. Initiating fire suppression program."

Kash sprinted off the bridge. Section nine was designated crew quarters. Compartment one belonged to the ship's commander. Him. Gwen was in danger.

It took him less than a minute to get to his quarters, but it was still too long. Gwen could be dead or injured, and it would be his fault.

He activated the door and charged inside, only to be met with a cloud of acrid smoke and even more acidic language.

"If you don't let me the fuck out of here, I swear to fucking god I'm going to set fire to...Finally!"

Gwen was standing by the door, drenched in fire-retardant foam streaked with soot.

"You are unhurt?" He grabbed her and folded her into his arms, running his hands over every inch of her body, looking for injuries.

"No thanks to you! You left. You locked me in your room and left after you promised not to. And then I was mad, and the stupid door wouldn't open, and the computer kept yelling at me in Pyrosian and then *fwoosh!* Flames everywhere." She flung out her hands, sending gobs of foam flying.

"There was an emergency on the bridge, *kaheya*. I had to go. I'm sorry. I should have come back sooner."

She glowered up at him, iridescent foam sliding off her dark skin to reveal she was naked underneath. "You shouldn't have broken your promise to me. At the very least, you could have woken me up to tell me why you were leaving. "

Her small hand slapped against his chest. "You're a jerk. A big, sexy jerk. And I want to be mad at you, but I can't because this stupid Scorching thing is making me crazy. I hurt, Kash. And I set things on fire. How did I do that?"

She was trembling now, her curvy body rubbing against his. It was hard to think past the lust fogging his brain, but he owed her answers. Gods, he owed her so much more than that. "I don't know. You're human. None of this should be possible. I thought you would be less affected by the Scorching as I was. I thought I was the only one who would suffer if we stayed apart."

"Why were you away from her, Commander? I am certain I ordered you to stay with your mate until the Scorching was over." Torel appeared in the doorway, his features twisted into a disapproving scowl. Even displeased, he remembered to speak in English so Gwen could understand.

Kash tucked Gwen behind him, blocking Torel's view of his naked mate. "Get out, Torel. My mate is unclothed."

The medical officer stopped, then took a step backward, gesturing to whoever was behind him to stay back. "I can see you stayed away too long. Are you in control? How's the pain?"

"Barely, and bearable," Kash replied.

"No, and it hurts!" Gwen called out from behind

him. "I did this, so I'd say it's pretty clear I'm not in control. And what do you mean, you ordered him to stay with me?"

Her small fists hammered on his back, fueled by frustration but not real anger. "You had to be ordered to stay with me, and you left anyway?"

"Vadir's ship is missing. I was coordinating the search."

Her hands stilled. "Lisa?"

"Is with Vadir. We'll find them. I—" He was about to make another promise, but he stopped. She had no reason to trust his word. Not after what he'd done.

"You should have told me." She placed a trembling hand on his arm and moved so that she could peek up at him, her golden eyes wide with worry.

Torel gasped. "Her eyes!"

Kash barely managed to control his urge to hurt the other male for daring looking at Gwen. "Are gold. And she summoned the flames on her own. Her Pyrosian genetics have become dominant, which is something that will have to be discussed -- later."

"Of course. You're going to need new quarters. I'll arrange matters."

"Do that."

"And make sure they're fireproof. I don't know how to control whatever the hell is happening to me."

Torel grinned. "Avoid strong emotions, and you should be fine, Gwen. The Gods would not have granted you these powers if you could not handle them."

"Avoid strong emotions? Have you met the man I'm mated to?"

"I have. And I wish you good luck." The door closed, but not before he heard Torel's guffaws of laughter. The officer was going to pay for that at some point. For now, though...

He turned and wrapped his arms around Gwen again, hauling her in close. "What do you need from me, *kaheya*?"

"I need you to listen to me. Listen, and try to understand."

He hadn't expected that response. He wanted to do something for her. Make her promises, fix her hurts. Take some action that would make things right.

"What do I need to hear? Are you going to tell me what I can do to fix this?"

She uttered a soft sigh. "I don't need you to fix me. I need you to *hear* me."

He caught the frustration in her voice and worked to calm his mind. She had asked for his attention. He'd give it to her, even if it didn't feel like that was enough.

"I am listening."

"My father died before I was born. He was a soldier, and he died fighting in a war far from home. My mother died of cancer when I was still a little girl. Then, a few years later, my grandmother died. The people I care about keep leaving me. I'm afraid that I'm going to spend my life alone because no one will stay with me. Even Lisa and Maggie are leaving. I knew it would happen someday. They'd fall in love and move on, but I wasn't expecting them to go so far, or at the same time!"

"I'm not leaving you, Gwen. I can't. It would be like cutting out part of myself."

She tensed. "You did leave, though. You left me alone in a strange place without so much as a note. The door was locked, the computer wouldn't answer me, and you were gone. Well, mostly gone. I could still sense you a little, but it wasn't enough."

"I was an *akinu*. A fool. It won't happen again."

"But why? You could have told me you had to go. I would have understood."

She was looking up at him with such pain in her eyes that his heart cracked open and the truth poured out. "All my life, I have fought to be recognized for my own merits. Duty and honour were everything to me because I had earned those for myself. Then, I met you, and for the first time in my life, I felt like I had to choose. Duty, or you. I didn't know how to do that."

You really are an, what did you say, an *akinu*? You didn't have to choose. You could have told me what was happening and left. That's my friend you're looking for. Did you think I'd stop you?"

He didn't have an answer to that, and it must have been obvious by his expression because his little mate shook her head and sighed.

"Men. Some things are the same no matter what their species. You're making this more complicated than it has to be. You're my mate, right? That means you need to talk to me and tell me what you're thinking."

"Yes. You are my mate. You are my everything, Gwen Hudson. I can feel you, here." He tapped his chest. "And I heard you, here." He raised his hand to touch his temple. "I was on my way back to you before the fire alarm sounded. I felt your unhappiness. I'm sorry I was the cause."

"Apology accepted." She looked around at the scorch marked walls and charred furniture. "I'm really sorry about your stuff."

"Things can be replaced. You can't. When I realized the fire was in my quarters when I thought you might be hurt, or worse...Flames, I've never run so fast in my life."

"Flames. Yeah. There were lots of those." She swiped at a trickle of foam that dripped down her cheek. "And then there was foam everywhere. For the record, this stuff tastes awful."

He chuckled and bent his head to kiss her. When she rose up on her toes to meet him halfway, the ache in his heart finally started to fade. She'd forgiven him.

The second his lips touched hers, the Scorching came back with such fury that he groaned aloud, the sound muffled against the soft lines of her mouth. Lust poured through him, burning away any thought but the need to lay claim to her, body and soul. He plunged his tongue into her mouth, savouring the pleasure of having her back in his arms. Why had he stayed away from her so long? He couldn't remember the reason, but he knew he wouldn't make the same mistake again.

Their kiss deepened. The heat between them blooming into a firestorm of primal needs and wants. Not even the bitter taste of the foam that coated her face could distract him from the sweet taste of her lips, though it did make her naked body slick and hard to hold.

"Hang onto me. It's time I got you cleaned up."

"Took you long enough," she whispered, her arms twining around his neck.

That observation could easily sum up his entire day. He'd been slow to accept everything about her. Her existence. His need for her. What she meant to his future. He was done taking things slow.

He carried her through the foam-soaked wreckage of the room to the hygiene alcove. It had been spared any serious damage, both from her flames and from the ship's automated response.

"Computer, activate cleansing compartment. Water temperature two degrees below my usual setting. And dial back the pressure by fifteen percent."

"It can do all that with a shower?" Gwen reached out to cut a handful of water as it began to fall from the ceiling and cascade like a curtain of rain.

"I haven't made time to show you the wonders of

your new life. It's one more thing I need to make up to you."

"That's getting to be a long list. You really should get on with making things up to me, or we might never make it through it all."

He dropped his communicator on the counter and stepped into the shower without bothering to undress. "That is exactly what I intend to do."

7

———

"You're still dressed!"

"Not for long. I'm going to try undressing your way. The water is to make sure I don't set off the fire suppression system again."

"Don't you da—"

He kissed her before she could finish her sentence, and the next thing she knew, they were surrounded by fire. The water hissed as it struck the wall of flames, and the air quickly filled with steam. His uniform turned to ash and washed away, though he had to set her down to strip off the last few rags that were too wet to ignite.

"Efficient, but destructive. We're both going to run out of clothes at this rate."

He laughed, a deep, rumbling sound that fired her blood and made her clit throb. It was the sexiest noise she'd ever heard. "I'll switch to fireproof uniforms from now on. I can't protect the Prince with my new abilities if every time I do, I wind up naked."

"No one sees you naked but me. You might not be interested in other women, but any human female who sees you in all your glory is going to try her best to change your mind."

"My glory is for you alone." He crowded in close, pressing her into the corner of the shower stall. "As yours is only for me."

"Only yours," she agreed, the words filling her with joy. Her grandmother had loved her. Her friends had defended her, but no one in her life had ever made her feel the way Kash did. Protected. Cherished. Maybe someday, even loved. Despite their rocky start, she could see that happening. God knew she was more than a little in love with the big jerk already.

The fiery need blazing through her when she'd woken up had quieted when he'd first arrived. Just having him touch her had been enough to sooth the ache for a little while. Now that they were alone, the mating fever returned in force.

She ran her hands over his body, hunger warring with admiration as she explored him for the first time. He was built on a scale that made her feel tiny. She stroked the broad expanse of his shoulders down to the first true six-pack abs she'd ever seen in real life. Then she worked her way lower, wrapping her hand around the hard shaft of his cock as she lowered herself to her knees in front of him.

"*Kaheya*, you should not be on your knees in front of me. If anything, it should be me worshipping at your feet, seeking forgiveness."

"We're both going to make mistakes. This is new to both of us, right? Maybe we should start a tradition of apologizing with orgasms." Her cheeks burned hotter than the steam as she spoke, but her embarrassment faded when he gave her a hot-eyed nod.

"Yes. I like this idea."

Feeling more wanton than she'd ever been in her life, she leaned and wrapped her lips around his cock, humming softly as she reached up to cup his balls in one hand. She pumped his shaft with her other hand, and he uttered a low groan of need. He leaned back against the wall, his hips rocking lightly. Strong fingers tangled in her curls, holding her head steady as he slowly fucked her mouth.

Warm water fell in a sensual rain that caressed her bare skin and amplified every physical sensation. She could taste the subtle musk of his skin, and every breath drew that same scent deep into her lungs. His fingers tightened in her hair as he groaned again, this one edged with need.

She took him deeper into her mouth, teasing him with her lips, tongue, and teeth. When he bucked his hips, she hollowed her cheeks and sucked until his balls tightened beneath her fingers and his thighs tensed.

"If you don't stop, you're going to bring me to my

knees whether you want me there or not," he warned her.

She raised her head, releasing his cock to speak. "Then you better hang onto something because I'm not done with you, yet."

He muttered something that had to have been a Pyrosian curse of some kind and then gripped a small shelf she hadn't noticed before. It was the same material as the walls, and it held an assortment of bottles and what looked like some kind of soap.

She tightened her grip on the root of his shaft and began pumping as she bowed her head and took him to the back of her mouth before easing back again. She circled the crown of his cock with her tongue, learning what spots made him quiver with need. It was empowering to have such a strong man in her thrall like this, and she was enjoying every second of it.

Only when his breath was coming in ragged groans did she finally open her mouth and take him deep, swallowing as much of him as she could. She let him rest at the back of her throat as she swallowed several times in rapid succession. It was enough to push him over the edge. He came with a shout, pouring his cum down her throat.

There was a loud crack and a crash as something hit the floor of the shower. She opened her eyes and giggled as she spotted the remains of the shelf he'd been gripping lying a few feet away.

She ran her tongue over him one last time, then

released him. "We've finished the job. Every room in your quarters is now officially wrecked."

"Indeed." He helped her to her feet, then hauled her into his arms for a kiss that stole her breath and sent shockwaves coursing through her.

It wasn't only the kiss that had her reeling. It was the emotion behind it. She could sense him, his feelings and needs. He craved her, but it was more than that. There was amazement, and happiness, and a yearning that she recognized as a twin to her own deepest desires.

Soulmate. She'd read a thousand stories that used the word, but until this moment, she hadn't understood what it truly meant.

"I feel you," she whispered, lifting her hand to touch her temple the way he had earlier.

"And I feel you. Our bond is growing stronger. We'll always be linked now."

"I'll never be alone again?"

"Never." He cupped her cheek in his hand and smiled down at her with such joy it made her heart sing. "We are one."

"I like the sound of that."

"You'll like what comes next even more. I promise." He lifted her into his arms, his mouth slanting across hers as he turned and carried her to an undamaged corner of the shower.

She wrapped her legs around his hips as he pressed her into the wall and held her there as he kissed her again and again. Every touch was a primal claiming, skin to skin, mouths mated, breath mingled. She moaned and arched against him, craving the feel of his body against hers.

It wasn't long before his cock began to harden again as they ground against each other. Their movements grew more frenzied as need overtook them. She pulled herself high enough that his cock slid between the lips of her pussy. Both of them moaned as he stroked his length over her swollen clit.

"I need you," she whispered against his lips.

"Then take me."

He rocked his hips and shifted his grip so their bodies could come together. The thick head of his cock breached her entrance with a slow, steady thrust that didn't end until he was fully sheathed inside her.

She clung to him, her face buried in the side of his neck as he took her hard, the wet slap of skin on skin and the scent of sex filling the air. He loved her with a wild passion that set her world ablaze. Every nerve tingled, and pleasure flowed through her as he stretched her body to accommodate his.

She muffled her cries against his throat, her nails raking across his shoulders as the pleasure grew.

He groaned her name as he pounded into her, every stroke harder and faster than the one before. They left their marks on each other: nail scores and teeth marks, swollen lips and beard-reddened cheeks.

"Look at me when you come." His gruff words

made her lift her head, and she stared into eyes that glowed like molten gold. There was adoration in his gaze, and she could sense his feelings through the bond they shared. It wasn't love, not yet, but it would be.

She came apart in his arms, soaring on a wave of bliss that carried her to the stars and back. He bellowed her name seconds later, his cock jerking as he came. When he thickened inside her, locking them together, the pressure was enough to trigger another orgasm, and she shuddered and gasped as her body milked his.

Sated and finally sane, she let herself slump against him. Her head rested on his shoulder, her arms dangling limply around his neck. "Shower sex good."

He chuckled. "Yes, it is. Remind me to be sure our new quarters have a nice, big shower so we can do that often."

"We should probably make sure the shelves are sturdy, too." She waved a hand in the vague direction of the wrecked shelf he'd broken early. "Wait, we're getting new quarters? Why?"

"Because I currently live in the barracks. My position comes with quarters at the palace, but I have never chosen to live there."

"No barracks." Gwen had spent time in foster homes that operated that way. She remembered the lack of privacy, the whispers, the cruel jokes when there were no adults around to intervene. Dorm-style living was not something she ever wanted to experience again.

"Will we really live at the palace? Will Maggie be there? Oh god, I'm going to have to meet the king and queen, aren't I? I mean, at some point, that's going to happen, right?"

"You have started asking your questions in bunches again. You must be feeling better."

"I am. And you didn't answer any of my questions."

"First, we need to get out of here, dry off, and move to a room that wasn't recently set on fire. Then, I will answer your questions."

"Throw in some food, and you have yourself a deal."

"Food will be arranged, and before we go, we can see if your cookies survived."

"Shit. The cookies! And my phone. And my purse! This fire summoning thing is going to be expensive."

"Whatever you need, I'll get it for you." His mouth quirked into a smile. "I am not a rich man, but I am not poor, either. I will see to it you have all you need."

Gwen's legs could hardly hold up her weight by the time she left the shower. The all-consuming need of the Scorching had finally quieted, leaving her sated and spent. She leaned against the counter as Kash dried her with a thick, plush towel that seemed to soak in the water as soon as it came in contact with it. He tended to her with care, seeing to every inch of her body, right down to her hair. He seemed fascinated with her curls, coiling them around his fingers as they dried into their usual tight spirals.

"My sister is going to be envious of your hair. Never have I seen curls like yours."

"They're a pain in the neck most of the time. Growing up, I always wanted straight, flowing hair like the other girls I knew."

"And when I was a youngling I wanted to be smaller. I was always the biggest of the young males. I hated it. It made me stand out when all I wanted was to be invisible." He touched his face. "Once I got these it got even worse. People didn't just notice me, they went out of their way to avoid me."

She laid her hand over his. "Then they're idiots. But I do understand. Some humans don't feel comfortable around anyone different from them. Skin colour. Language. Customs. Scars. I was born with dark skin. It's not something I chose. But it bothers them anyway."

He nodded, then turned his head to kiss the inside of her wrist. "My species is much older than yours, but we still struggle with some things. Your skin colour, though, will not be an issue on Pyros."

"No? Well, that will be a refreshing change."

"So, if colour and culture aren't issues anymore,

what do Pyrosians struggle with? Is this part of why you wanted to be invisible when you were young?"

"It is. And I'll tell you about it once I have you back in bed again. The only thing holding you up right now is that counter."

This time when he lifted her, she didn't feel a single twinge of concern about her weight. He accepted her as she was. More than that. He cared for her. Somehow, they were going to make this work.

Kash wrapped them both in towels before entering the corridor and making his way to their new quarters. It was only across the hall from their current location, and he had Gwen back behind closed doors in a matter of seconds.

"Wow. We got an upgrade," Gwen muttered as she looked around.

"These rooms are normally reserved for the royal family and their guests."

"So, you get practical and utilitarian, and they get...this? I'm afraid to touch anything in here in case I set it on fire. I'm betting those sheets cost more than you make in a month. And is that bedspread velvet?"

"Torel would have ensured that everything in here is fireproof. There's no risk of damage. We are not the first couple to initiate the Scorching while on a space vessel." There were protocols in place. Protocols that he had forgotten about.

Her soft hand cupped his cheek. "You look like someone just kicked your puppy. What's bothering you?"

"I should have initiated certain protocols for us – for you – before I left."

"If I were Pyrosian, then sure. But how could you have known I was suddenly going to turn into a super-hero and *fwoosh*? And you never lose control, so why would you need it?"

"Is that what you think, that I never lose control?" He carried her over to the bed and settled her carefully atop the sumptuous bedspread.

"Mhmm. You're the most disciplined man I've ever met. You're all about duty, and honour, and ensuring that everything goes exactly the way it's supposed to." She nestled against the soft fabric and then patted the empty space at her side. "Why is that?"

"You're wrong about that. I used to be disciplined. Then I saw your picture on my monitor. From that moment on, I had no control. I ignored the orders given for the mission and came to Earth. I broke more rules when I told you who I was, and where your friends were. I defied a royal command to take you as my mate, and if I had the chance to do it all over again, I know I'd make the same choices. You have broken me, *kaheya*. When it comes to you, I have no control at all."

He stripped away the towels and stretched out beside her on the bed. She curled up beside him before he was even fully settled. He liked how it felt. She didn't fear him. There was no pity in her eyes when she looked at him. There was only admiration and desire...and occasionally irritation, but he had earned that.

"That might be the nicest thing anyone has ever said to me. But that's not the answer I wanted. I asked you why you need to control everything. Why are you so concerned with duty? I've seen the way the others look at you. They follow your orders without question. They trust and like you. You've already earned their respect. Believe me, I know what that looks like. So why are you still trying so hard?"

"My mother asks me the same question. She is going to like you, very much." He wrapped an arm around her and turned his head to kiss the crown of her hair. "My father is the High Commander of the armies of Pyros. I have lived my life in the shadow of his accomplishments. I had to work twice as hard to prove that I earned every promotion and accolade I was given because there was always someone who would say I only got it because of who my father was."

"Surely they don't say that anymore? I mean, look at what you've made of yourself."

"The habits of a lifetime are hard to break. And I've never had a reason to try. Not until you came along." He toyed with her curls as they talked, amazed at how content he felt simply holding her. He never talked to anyone like this. Well, no one but his family.

"I'll do my best to remind you that you're already pretty damned amazing so long as you keep saying such sweet things. You make me feel special. Like I...I matter."

He rose up on one elbow to stare down at her. "Of course you matter. Flames and fury, you're my mate! No one matters more than you do. Not my parents, or my sister, or even the royal family I'm sworn to defend." The moment he said the words, he recognized the truth behind them, and something clicked into place deep within his soul. Nothing mattered more than she did. Nothing ever would.

"Let's not mention that to them, hmm? I love that you feel that way, but if I have to meet your family and the king and queen, I'd rather not have them know where your priorities lie. It might make things awkward, and I really want them to like me."

"They will like you. You are smart, generous, and your spirit is as beautiful as your smile. You represent the future of our race."

Her smile faded. "You're talking about children. I was rejected from the dating site because I'm too old for that. Remember?"

"The Gods brought us together for a reason. Maybe it includes having younglings, or maybe not. We'll find out the answer to that in time. I have you, and that's enough for me."

"Will it be enough for your family?"

"Not even my father would dare question the will of the Gods. You are my mate. That is all they have ever wanted for me."

She exhaled softly. "You're probably going to have to remind me of that a fair bit. I'm not used to being what anyone wants. Well, except for Maggie and Lisa, but they're different. They're my family."

"You're my family now, too." He wasn't sure how to do it, but he tried to open his mind to her and let her sense the feelings she stirred inside him. When her smile returned, he knew he'd succeeded.

He had a new mission, now. For the rest of his life, he'd do everything he could to make sure she always smiled at him that way.

8

─────────

Gwen lay in bed, surrounded by luxuries and comforts she never thought she'd experience. The furnishings were sumptuous, soft, and molded to her body to make even the act of sitting into a sinful experience. The dark red décor had just enough gold and other pale colours interjected to be lovely without being overpowering. Even the lighting was a soft, buttery yellow. If this was a taste of what life in the palace would be like, then she was going to live a very pampered, comfortable life.

Kash was spending a few minutes on the bridge, and she was using the time to practice wrapping her tongue around the unfamiliar sounds that made up the Pyrosian language. Kash had tasked Torel with ensuring that the cognitive augmentation programs were safe for her to use. Once that happened, she'd been learning all she could about their language and culture between bouts of mind-blowing sex with Kash.

Kash. Just thinking about him made her smile. The Scorching was almost over, but her feelings for him hadn't diminished in the last two days. They'd grown stronger every hour, as had the bond they shared. His presence was always with her, and she reveled in the idea that she would never be alone again.

She felt the now familiar buzz that heralded his close proximity, and seconds later he came charging into their quarters, grinning from ear to ear.

"We found them."

"Lisa and Vadir? Are they alright? Where the hell have they been?"

"They crashed, as we suspected. They're both fine, and Lisa has been very concerned about you. She wanted me to tell you that she's sorry she couldn't let you know she was alright." His grin widened. "I told her I would pass that information along to you."

"Oh my god. You told her I was here? Do they know about us? What did she say?"

"Slowly, my love. One question at a time."

"You can command a starship, but you can't keep track of more than one question?" she rose from the bed and bounced over to him, relief making her foot-steps light.

"Of course I can, but I've discovered that your nose wrinkles in the cutest way when you're annoyed with me, and I wanted to see it again."

"You're impossible! Answer, me, please."

He wrapped her into his arms and held her close. "Vadir noticed my eyes, and Lisa guessed who I was mated to right away. She seemed very pleased and quite proud of herself for arranging for the three of you to sign up. I believe she said she was taking credit for the way things worked out."

Gwen laughed. "She would say that. When will they be here? Do Joran and Maggie know?"

"Joran contacted me while I was speaking with Vadir and Lisa. He and Maggie are at your residence. I made a request for them to bring you some of your things."

"You did? Thank you! I'd kill for some hair product to tame these curls, and it would be nice to be in my own clothes again." Kash had provided her with clothing made from flame resistant fabric, but she hadn't had much of a chance to wear them while they were in the thrall of the Scorching. The fabric was stiff and strange against her skin, too. She was dying to get back into a pair of faded jeans and a nice, comfy sweatshirt.

"Your curls are beautiful, just like the rest of you. I cannot wait to introduce you to Vadir and Joran. They are going to be amazed that the Gods gifted me with such an incredible female."

"Just promise me I don't have to meet your parents just yet."

"They are happy to wait. As eager as they are to

speak with you, they understand this has been a surprise for us both. We'll talk to them once we are on our way home."

"You mean after we leave Earth forever." She hadn't expected to be sad about leaving. The only people she cared about were going to Pyros with her. She was taking the few belongings she owned that mattered to her, like the cookie tin and her grandmother's recipe book. But it still bothered her to think that she could never come back.

"That might not be the case anymore. Your friend claims she's found a workaround that would negate the Council's laws. Vadir believes it will work so it could be that you'll be able to come back. Knowing Vadir, he's probably already working on plans to build a vast trade network with your planet."

"You're full of good news today. When are they getting here? I can't wait to see them, and meet the guys they're mated to. Do I have to bow to the prince or anything?"

"We're going to meet them on the surface. Vadir's ship still needs some parts and final repairs before it can fly again. I'll assist, along with Joran and his guards, while you catch up with your friends."

"We're going? When?"

He ran a hand down her spine to cup her bare ass. "That depends on whether you want to have sex in our bed, or in the cockpit of the shuttle once we're underway."

Feeling indecently wicked, she grabbed his shoulders and hopped upward, knowing that he'd catch her. "Why can't we do both?"

"Because we're going to be late if we do that."

"Then they can start the repairs without us. For once, I vote we do what we want and not worry about what anyone else thinks."

Heat flared in his eyes as he caught and lifted her high enough to kiss her. "Just this once."

She hummed in agreement, but she knew this wouldn't be the last time they broke the rules. She made him lose control, and he gave her the courage to reach for things she thought were beyond her reach.

EPILOGUE

(One Year Later)

Gwen sat out in the small but private garden that had come with their new apartment within the palace. The sky overhead was a paler blue than the one she'd known on Earth, but after a year of living on Pyros, she'd grown accustomed to the differences. The stars that filled the night sky may not be the ones she'd grown up with, but they were still beautiful, and the twin moons that orbited this world made for some truly amazing moonlit nights.

Sometimes, it felt like only a few days had passed since she had been reunited with Maggie and Lisa. That first meeting had been memorable. They had hugged and babbled incessantly, alternating between laughter and tears as they caught each other up on the momentous events of their time apart. Lisa had been gleeful about how well her suggestion to try the Star-Crossed dating site had worked out, and Maggie had repeatedly demanded her friends' solemn word that they would help her step into her new role as a princess. Gwen's golden eyes and new abilities amazed everyone, including her friends' new mates.

Meeting the powerful men who had claimed Lisa and Maggie's hearts had been nerve wracking, but that feeling hadn't lasted long. They looked at her friends with the same adoration as Kash looked at her, which made it easy to like them. By the time they arrived on Pyros, the six had become fast friends, full of hope and plans for not only their futures, but the future of both their races.

Her infant daughter burbled softly and stirred, drawing Gwen's attention down to the tiny miracle in her arms. Hope had been born two months ago, and the entire planet had celebrated her arrival. She was the first child to be born to any of the human/Pyrosian pairings, and the only female to be born on the planet in nearly five years.

"Hello, sweet pea. Did you have a good nap?" she cooed, her heart overflowing with love for her little girl.

"Of course she did. She's resting up so she can cry at maximum volume for hours tonight when her parents are trying to sleep."

Gwen turned to see Kash standing in the doorway

with a smile on his handsome face. "You're back. How did the meeting go?"

"It would have gone much faster if everyone wasn't asking after you and Hope. Lilanna was disappointed you weren't in attendance. It was all I could do to stop her from sending someone to escort you to the meeting. She insists that you come to the next one."

"And when Hope gets fussy?"

Kash walked over to where she sat and crouched at her side, his big hands stroking his daughter's cheek as he leaned in and kissed Gwen. "To quote our beloved queen, 'anyone who complains about Hope can bring it up with me, and I will tell them what I think of their priorities.' I don't think we'll have any trouble."

"The only trouble we'll have is getting our daughter back from Lilanna afterward. She's quite smitten with our little angel."

"Along with the rest of the planet."

"That'll change soon enough. Maggie's due in four months. When the princess gives birth, everyone will forget about us. I'm starting to think Lisa was the smart one. She's gallivanting about the galaxy with Vadir right now, having the time of her life."

"I know you don't mean that. You wouldn't give up our Hope for anything in the universe, and neither would I. It will be easier once we're on our way to Earth. Joran and I have already decided that we're going to stretch out the journey as long as we can and turn it into something of a vacation. We'll have Isli with us to help with Hope, too. Vadir and Lisa will meet up with us before we use the rift generator to make the hop to the far side of the galaxy."

"That sounds nice. Are we going on the *Firebrand*?" She had fond memories of that ship. After all, it was where Hope had been conceived. Birth control pills don't work when you don't take them for several days, and thanks to the Scorching, she hadn't even thought about it until they returned to her house to pack up her things.

"We are. Along with two other vessels that will carry the males selected for this miss— I mean, this round of pairings."

A lot had changed since she and the others had been quietly whisked away from Earth. There were no more missions to sneak in and steal human women. It had taken time to convince the Inter-Planetary Council that the existence of Pyrosian DNA in the human population was proof that first contact had already been made, but Vadir had used his considerable influence to maintain the pressure until the Council had agreed. Thanks to Lisa's idea, Earth was entering a new phase, one that might save both the people and the planet a great deal of suffering.

"What was the final count?" Originally, Gwen had been part of the planning process, but since Hope's birth, she had stepped back and allowed others to take over. Today's meeting had been the first of several to finalize the details of the next part of the adventure.

"Five hundred and thirty-seven males have been matched and will be accompanying us to Earth."

"That many? The last I heard it was only three hundred or so."

"The information campaign we're running on Earth is starting to work. More females have signed up to be tested in the last few weeks. By the time we bring the first group home, there may well be enough matches to send more ships. Once they meet you and the other females already living on Pyros and hear your stories, I imagine that we'll have more volunteers than Earth's governments were counting on. There might be some resistance once they realize what's happening."

"If they are true mates, it won't matter what the governments want. They all signed the same agreement. No technology or trade unless they agreed to allow any woman who voluntarily signed up to be taken to Pyros if she is matched." And the governments had agreed so quickly she'd wondered if they'd even read the whole agreement. Some of them probably hadn't, but that was their problem.

Earth was now a probationary member of the Council, and they had quickly come to realize that their newly discovered neighbours were more advanced than humans in every way. If they wanted access to the technology and knowledge to stabilize their world, end hunger, and create a brighter future for everyone, then they were going to have to play by the Council's rules.

"You are adorable when you're being fierce. Of course, they'll abide by the agreement. Just as the application process here is open to any unmated male, regardless of their age or status."

"Maggie made sure of that. For someone who aspired to live a small, simple life, she's certainly adapted well to life as a future queen. She's really the fierce one. I just stood back and watched her work."

"You did so much more than that. I am proud of all you have accomplished, *kaheya*. And now you will return to your planet and be hosted by the leaders of your world."

She groaned. "Don't remind me. The only reason I'm doing this is because I know you'll be at my side. I'm still not sure how I got talked into this."

He leaned in, resting his head against her shoulder as he stared down at Hope with a goofy smile on his face. "You were the obvious choice. Maggie is still learning her duties as the next queen, and Lisa is with Vadir, helping him negotiate his trade agreements with Earth. But even if they weren't already busy, you would still be the perfect one to take this role."

"You're biased."

"Yes, I am. But I am still right. You were born to do this, and I will be with you the whole time. If it gets to be too much, just hold up this beautiful little girl and let her charm them all."

"She is pretty charming, isn't she? She must get that from me."

Kash snorted. "Are you saying I'm not charming? I managed to convince you to come away with me to live on another planet, didn't I?"

"Yeah, but you made me so mad I set your room on fire, first. Plus, you had divine intervention working in your favour."

"Yes, I did. And I give thanks to the Gods every day for it. I didn't know how empty my life was until you came along and showed me what I was missing."

She let all the love and joy in her heart well up inside her, and let it flow through the bond that would connect them for the rest of their lives. She'd found her future, her family, and her home the night Kash had knocked at her door.

Soon, she would go back to Earth and offer the same opportunity to other women who dreamed of finding someone to love. After all, she was now the spokeswoman for the Star-Crossed Dating Service. Offering adventure and romance from out of this world was all part of her job description.

THE END

ABOUT THE INTERGALACTIC DATING AGENCY SERIES

Ready for more out of this world romances? The adventure isn't over yet! Fly over to our dating agency website to check out more stories from this multi-author series. The Intergalactic Dating Agency is ready and waiting to set you up with a host of alien hotties from all over the galaxy.

Make a date with your alien match today.

http://romancingthealien.com

Want to read more stories with book boyfriends that are out of this world?

Check out Susan Hayes' other Science Fiction Romance Titles

<u>The Drift</u>
Double Down
All In
Wild Card
Three of a Kind
No Limit

<u>Nova Force</u>
Operation Phoenix

<u>3013: The Series</u>
3013: RENEGADE
3013: STOWAWAY
3013: TARGETED
3013: FATED
3013: SCARRED

JORAN
Star-crossed Alien Mail Order Brides #1

What do you do when your planet runs out of women? Send for takeout, of course.

Joran, Crown Prince of Pyros, needs to claim his mate in order to ascend to the throne one day. The problem? His destined mate isn't on Pyros.

When a galaxy-wide search uncovers a backwater world full of potential mates for Joran and the other unmated males on his planet, plans are set in motion and Star-Crossed Dating is created. Now, the first wave of men are on their way to claim their unsuspecting brides. Joran's mission: Go to Earth, claim his mate and bring her back to Pyros. How hard could it be?

This book contains a redheaded barista who doesn't believe in aliens, and a prince who is used to getting anything he wants without having to work for it...until now.

A SNEAK PEAK AT JORAN

Maggie nestled into one side of her best friend's worn but comfy couch with a container of rocky road ice cream in one hand and a spoon in the other. After the week she'd had, ice cream and a girls' night in was exactly what she needed.

"Do we want to open the red or white wine?" Gwen called from the tiny, galley-style kitchen.

"Red. That's a good pairing for cookie dough ice cream, right?" Lisa said, already digging into her ice cream from her perch on the other side of the couch.

"Everything's a good pairing for cookie dough." Gwen reappeared with a bottle of red wine and three glasses on a tray, along with her preferred flavor, chocolate ripple.

Gwen served the wine and then settled into a somewhat battered armchair with a contented sigh and raised her glass. "We survived another week. Here's to the weekend."

"Amen," Maggie replied, before downing a significant portion of her glass.

"Uh oh. You only drink your wine that fast when the espresso machine at work is on the fritz or you're having man trouble. Which is it?"

Maggie wrinkled her nose and sighed. "The latter. Jorge went back to his wife."

Gwen's hand froze, her spoon hovering halfway between the carton and her mouth. "Wife? I thought you said he was divorced?"

"He is. Well, he was. They finalized the divorce three years ago." Maggie took another drink, but the wine couldn't wash away the bitter taste that had lingered in her mouth since she got the text from Jorge the night before.

"Weren't you two planning a romantic getaway next weekend? How the hell does a guy go from booking a trip with his girlfriend to getting back together with his ex-wife?" Lisa leaned over to snag the bottle of wine off the table and refilled Maggie's glass.

"It was his turn with the kids last weekend. I guess he told them about me, and they went home and told their mother." Maggie paused to take another spoonful of ice cream while Lisa and Gwen reacted like the best friends that they were.

"He's an idiot. She doesn't want him back, she just wants to make sure he isn't with anyone else. The moment she finds out he dumped you, she'll call it off again. If he can't see that, he's not worthy of you," Maggie said, utterly indignant.

"Please, tell me you had a moment of glorious red-headed temper and tore him a new one before punting his sorry ass to the curb," Lisa added.

"He didn't give me the chance. He told me by text message late last night."

"He broke up with you by *text*? The least he could have done was tell you in person. What kind of man does that?" Maggie asked.

"The only kind of man the three of us ever seem to attract. Weak, selfish assholes." Lisa stabbed her spoon into her ice cream. "We need to expand our dating pool."

Maggie shook her head. "I'm not sure how we'd do that. I work in a coffee shop, which means the only guys I meet are over-caffeinated business types who never look up from their phones long enough to flirt. You're a street artist, so you're surrounded by buskers all day. Those guys barely make rent, they can't afford a girlfriend."

Lisa grinned. "No, but the cute ones can rent me for a couple of days. Not every relationship has to last forever."

Gwen rolled her eyes. "Some of us are getting too old to play the field. I'd like to meet someone special. He doesn't need to be perfect, just...perfect for me."

"You've spent too many years reading those

romance novels you love, Gwen. There's no such thing as a perfect man. He's a myth, like unicorns and little green men from outer space." Maggie took another drink of her wine. "I agree with Lisa though, we do need to find a better class of men to date. There has to be some out there, somewhere."

"Given our track records, maybe not. Between us, we've dated a card-carrying member of the Ghost-busters fan club, complete with his own proton pack, two guys who forgot they were still married..."

Gwen chimed in with "Don't forget the guy who met Lisa for coffee, talked about himself for an hour, then told her she was clearly a submissive and asked her to wear his collar...on their first date."

Lisa groaned. "Seth. Oh man, I'd forgotten about him. He was a wannabe Dom with no clue what he was talking about. Quick, someone pass me more wine. I'm going to need it to erase those memories again."

They spent the next hour drinking, laughing, eating ice cream, and reminiscing about their worst dating experiences. They'd been friends for so long they knew all the stories already, but that didn't matter. They still laughed at each other and tossed in the occa-sional reminder about a detail someone had missed. Usually something that made the whole tale even more humiliating. That's what friends were for.

Gwen and Lisa were more than friends, though. They were the sisters of her heart. They had been there for Maggie when she'd first landed in foster care as a broken and terrified twelve-year-old. Since then, the three of them had forged a friendship that had lasted twenty years.

"This might be the wine talking, but I think I'm ready to try online dating again," Lisa announced. "It's that or dye my hair. Whichever. It's time for a change."

"You have gorgeous hair. Do you know how many women would kill to be natural blondes?" Gwen tugged on a curl of her tightly spiraled, jet-black hair to make her point. "Me, for one."

"Then I'm taking your comment as a vote for a return to online dating. And so we're clear, I'm not going alone. You two are coming with me." Lisa grabbed her phone and started poking at the screen. "I got this email the other day. Some new dating site is coming online in the next few months, and they're looking for some brave souls to beta test it for free. Maybe we should give it a shot."

Maggie groaned. "You say that like you're going to give us a choice."

Lisa waved her hand around in vague circles. "What, and spoil the illusion? I like to let you guys think you have some say."

"We've been friends too long. That illusion got shattered years ago." Gwen drained her glass and then reached for her phone. "I can't believe I'm even considering this."

"Me, either." Maggie checked her email and quickly found the invite. Star-Crossed Dating Service.

A quick scan of the contents made her curious enough to click the link. The site looked professional enough. No spelling mistakes or weird links. She started to read, then stopped and read the same sentence over again.

"Am I reading this right? They offer a money back guarantee? If we're still single after six months, we get double our money back? I thought you said this was free?"

"Keep reading. In the next paragraph, they promise to pay us the cash, even as beta testers. They've got to be pretty confident to make that kind of offer," Lisa said.

"There has to be a catch." Gwen's expression darkened as she kept reading. "Young women looking for adventure and an out of this world dating experience. I'm not that young anymore, and I'm not sure I'm the adventurous type."

"You're thirty-four, not eighty. Come on, Gwen. Maybe your perfect-for-you guy is on this site, waiting to meet you. You'll never know unless you try." Lisa turned her gaze to Maggie. "So, what's your argument going to be?"

"I'm working on it. Give me a minute. I've had enough wine and ice cream that it's tough to think right now."

"Perfect. In that case, have another glass." Lisa held up the nearly empty wine bottle. "Drink up, then sign up. We're doing this."

"Bossy cow," Maggie muttered with a laugh as she held out her glass.

"Mooo 'betcha," Lisa retorted, and all three of them burst into a fit of giggles.

The laughter continued as they filled out the questionnaire for the dating site, each of them offering up suggestions on what the others should put. It was certainly more fun than doing it alone, but Maggie still didn't expect much in the way of results. When it came to dating, being skeptical kept her from getting her hopes dashed over and over again.

As a girl, she'd lived like a princess in a fairytale, but when her father died, she'd lost everything. Her friends. Her home. Even her mother. She'd learned her lesson. Now, Maggie kept her expectations low and her dreams small. It was safer that way. If this dating site was as good as it claimed to be, then maybe it would match her with a man who understood how to live the same way she did. Small and simple.

What do you do when your planet runs out of women? Send for takeout, of course.

Vadir has a business empire to run and no time to spare on frivolous endeavors. So how did he wind up on the far side of the galaxy to claim a mate he never signed up for? A matchmaking queen and a royal decree, that's how.

His plan is simple: meet the female, negotiate terms, and leave the primitive planet of Earth as fast as he can. What could possibly go wrong?

This book contains a bohemian blonde with a hell

of a right hook, and an interstellar tycoon who is about to learn that the best things in life can't be bought or sold, they have to be won.

A SNEAK PEAK AT VADIR

Vadir Rahal paced the floor of his office and tried to think of a way out of this insane predicament. He didn't have time for this right now. What was the King thinking?

Turning his back on the sweeping view of the city outside his windows, he stormed back to his desk and snatched the thick piece of parchment off the surface.

No one used parchment anymore. It had been an outdated concept two hundred years ago, but the royal family loved their traditions. The damned thing had even been delivered by a royal messenger in full uniform. He read the words again, looking for a loophole. Something, anything that he could use to decline the *honour* bestowed on him by the King and Queen of Pyros.

There wasn't one.

"By the Flames of the First One, why did it have to

be me?" he tossed the royal decree back onto the desktop and started pacing again.

"I've got a half-dozen deals to broker in the next week alone, and the Qualla Mining Consortium is threatening a work stoppage that could affect the ore markets for years to come. I need to be here, not on the other side of the galaxy retrieving my mate. I don't need a mate. I didn't ask for one. Crown Prince Joran is the one who needs a…"

He stopped in his tracks. Joran. If anyone could get him out of this, it would be the prince. He activated a wall monitor and called the one man on the planet who had any chance of changing the King's mind.

"So, I guess you got the decree?" Joran asked by way of greeting.

"You knew about this?"

The Prince nodded. "I'm going with you. Turns out, you're not the only one whose mate is supposedly on that planet."

"Why me? Is this because I refused to play nice with the Romakis during that last trade war? Is this your father's idea of revenge?"

"Wrong parent."

"Your *mother* did this to me? I thought she liked me!"

"She does. Which is why she insisted your profile be included when we screened for possible mates. The rest was luck, or if you believe my mother, the will of the Gods."

"So, this is real? My mate is out there?" The air in his perfectly maintained office suddenly seemed too thin.

"That's what the experts say. They may not be our true mates, but our scientists confirm we can have children with them."

"How can they possibly know that?"

Joran laughed. "I asked the same question. The answer is hard to believe, but I've seen the reports. Some of these people, humans, already carry Pyrosian genes."

"How?" Vadir demanded, too stunned by the revelation to manage more than a single word.

"I'll send you the report, and our experts' best guess as to how it happened. It makes for interesting reading, but the short version is, this is real."

"Our mates are out there, on another planet? And we're just going to wander over there, explain matters, and bring them back here? Do you know how insane that sounds?"

Joran nodded. "I know. Read the reports. You've got enough time to make whatever preparations are necessary, but you can't tell anyone where you're going. We'll figure out a cover story, probably something about you and I taking the *Firebrand* out on its maiden voyage to tour the system. Your shipyard built it, so no one will question why you're coming along."

"If you want it to be believable, I should bring my

private shuttle, too. Everyone knows I have control issues."

Joran snickered. "Fine, I'll leave room in the hangar for your ship. But don't think I don't know what you're doing. If you want to fly yourself down to the planet, you're going to need to clear that with Commander Denza. He's in charge of the mission."

Of course he was. Who else would the King entrust with the life of his son and heir? "I'll talk to him. I may have to obey this decree, but I'm not going to negotiate mating terms with some alien female surrounded by royal guardsmen. There are advantages to being me."

"Just be on board and on time." Joran grinned at him. "I'm sure you can negotiate the rest of the details to your satisfaction."

"I wouldn't dream of being late. An order is an order." And apparently, this was one command he wasn't going to be able to charm or buy his way around. Vadir recalled the final line of the missive he'd received. *You will go to Earth and determine if the female is your mate. If she is, then you are hereby commanded to bring her home to Pyros.* "I don't suppose I'm going to be allowed to do some trade negotiations while I'm there?"

Joran laughed at him. "Father said you'd ask, and his answer is no."

"I had to try."

"Of course you did. We'll talk again soon. I'll send you over the file with all the information we have on your match. It's not much, but at least you can see what she looks like. Her name is Lisa."

Joran signed off, leaving Vadir alone in his office.

I'm going to be mated. The thought hit him with the force of a rogue comet strike. He'd never imagined this day would come. Hadn't planned on it. Why would he, when there were so few unmated females on Pyros? He enjoyed the occasional dalliance with females from the planets he visited for business, but those were simple, short-term affairs. Taking a mate was anything but simple, which was why Vadir had hoped to avoid it. But not even his wealth and power allowed him to refuse a royal command.

Faced with a new challenge, Vadir did what he did best. He set aside his emotions and focused on making a plan. He'd been ordered to negotiate the biggest deal of his life, and failure was not an option. If the King and Queen wished him to bring back a mate, then that's what he'd do.

He needed to know as much about this Lisa as he could. Every being he'd ever met had a price. This female would be no exception. All he had to do was determine what she wanted, and offer it to her in exchange for leaving her primitive, isolated world to join him on Pyros and live in luxury for the rest of her life. It should be an easy sell.

———

Business had been slow all day, but that suited Lisa Woods just fine. She was still nursing a hangover from the wine she'd drunk last night. Or maybe it was an ice cream overdose. She pondered that idea for a moment and then rejected it. There was no such thing as too much ice cream.

There had definitely been too much wine, though. That's the only reason she had broken her vow to never go back to online dating. Apparently, four glasses were all it took to drown out the voice of reason. The proof was in her email inbox this morning: confirmation of registration to the Star-Crossed Dating Service.

At least she hadn't done it alone. She'd dragged Maggie and Gwen along with her on a quest for what the email promised would be an out-of-this-world dating experience.

"I could use a little out of this world," she mused to herself as she looked around. Vancouver was a beautiful city, but it was easy to forget that when you never got to compare it to anywhere else. Lisa had spent her whole life here, and she dreamed of taking off to explore the world someday. Someday was still a long way off, though, considering she barely earned enough money to eat and make her rent.

Lisa made her living drawing caricatures and quick sketches for tourists. It wasn't exactly a glamorous or high-paying job, especially when the tourists were few and far between. It was still early in the season, which meant the artists and street performers that dotted the seawall outnumbered their potential customers. She could head home to work on her paintings, but the spring sunshine was too nice to head indoors yet.

She sat underneath the canopy of her umbrella, idly sketching her surroundings when inspiration struck. She opened her sketch book to a fresh page and started drawing, the world around her fading away as she worked. Apart from the occasional pause to push her blonde hair back from her face, she stayed focused on the face taking shape on the paper.

Her mystery man had dark hair with a hint of curl in it, a strong jaw, and a mouth that curved up into an arrogant smile. Try as she might, she couldn't get his eyes right, though. She'd drawn them dark and brooding, staring back at her from beneath a lightly furrowed brow. She kept working at them, and then, in a flash of insight, she knew what was wrong. She reached out with a bare foot to snag the strap of her crocheted art supply bag and pulled it close enough that she could reach it without setting down the sketch book.

She fished out two of the artist's pens she used for signing her work and considered them for a moment. Gold or silver? She dropped the silver one back into her bag and quickly added a few gold highlights to her creation's eyes.

"Better." She stared at the face she'd drawn, wondering where her muse had drawn her inspiration from this time. It wasn't a face she recognized from television or the movies. And if she'd ever laid eyes on a man that good-looking in person, she'd damned sure wouldn't forget it. Especially not with those amazing eyes.

A breeze stirred, lifting her hair off her shoulders and ruffling the page of her book so that his eyes seemed to sparkle with silent amusement.

Lisa had long ago learned that when her muse took over like this, it was because the universe was trying to tell her something. Her friends teased her about it, but they knew it was true. After all, she'd drawn pictures of both Gwen and Maggie before they'd ever met. She'd drawn other things, too. Warnings that she had been too young and innocent to understand at the time. She wasn't innocent anymore, though. These days, when the universe whispered in her ear, she listened.

The wind came up again, lifting the hem of her skirt so that it swirled around her legs and sending goose bumps chasing down her spine. Something was coming. She stared down at the picture in her hands. Or *someone*.

ABOUT THE AUTHOR

Susan lives out on the Canadian west coast surrounded by open water, dear family, and good friends. She's jumped out of perfectly good airplanes on purpose and accidentally swum with sharks on the Great Barrier Reef.

If the world ends, she plans to survive as the spunky, comedic sidekick to the heroes of the new world, because she's too damned short and out of shape to make it on her own for long.

You can find out more about Susan and her books here:
www.susanhayes.ca